AFTER THE RAIN

STORIES THAT BIND US

ASHA IYER KUMAR

Made with ♥ on the Notion Press Platform
www.notionpress.com

To

my husband

who encourages me

to

follow my heart

Contents

Acknowledgements

First, to all my cheerleaders and readers who make me want to keep writing, thank you. Second, to my editor, Rima Kar Ghosh, who made the stories spanking clean with her exemplary editing skills. Without her, my stories will have remained just manuscripts.

CHAPTER ONE

After the Rain

It must have rained all night.

The dampness and the lingering chill in the air confirm my assumption that it indeed was yet another night of severe pounding from the heavens.

The rains this season have been relentless as the newspapers say – many people dead, many more missing; immense damage to property; and mayhem in the city. All tragedies from which I remain insulated, thanks to my secluded living.

I have only nuggets of information about the outside world and I nibble on them with scant regard and concern. Ensconced in my apartment on the fifteenth floor, I spare no thought for the rest of the world from which I have consciously withdrawn. There is nothing out there that evinces my interest or anyone who can evoke old, forgotten sentiments. But the frailty of this morning makes me inquisitive about the world outside and I gingerly push the sliding window open.

I realise that these days I have to exert more pressure than before, to slide the window. It could be that the rains have made the frame a little obstinate or that my reflexes were on their way to senile retardation.

I feel a sudden burst of city air in my face as the windows finally slide open. It brings with it all that this city, which has been my sanctuary for years now, stands for: the irrepressible doggedness, bravado and frostiness. I peer at the wet expanse outside my window, unabashed and sensuous in its swirls. I stretch my hand, touch its fragile form, and run my fingers over it gently as if on a lyre, in the same manner as lovelorn heroes did on my sprinkler-drenched body in innumerable films.

The breeze brings with it a gust of the past as I rest my head on the window frame and briefly relive some reels of my life from the yore. It makes me smirk, partly with satisfaction and partly with contempt.

I remember the days when heroes who had an opportunity to brush their hands on me in front of the camera, harboured a secret desire to plunder the opulence of my youth behind closed doors. I have seen their lustful eyes expose their desire and their hesitant, faltering hands longing to linger on my skin for an extended moment of celluloid romance. I smile as I think of how willingly I basked in the glory of being the darling of the industry: ravishing, resplendent and utterly inaccessible to ordinary tinsel men.

Producers openly acknowledged that I had a price that was prohibitive, yet they scrambled to get me to sign up for their projects. Men from the industry drooled at my thought and made ludicrous overtures that I discreetly dodged. My elusiveness made them lust after me more feverishly than before. And how silly it made them look in front of me. The kind of things they said and did!

'Seemaji, do you know that the men in our country are suffering from unstoppable wet dreams? What are you going to do about it?' an inebriated journalist once asked me at a party.

I laughed throwing my head back, pushed a vagrant lock of hair behind my ears, and merely said, 'I know,' and moved on. It was my way of cocking a snook at the impudence of such filthy-mouthed men.

Behind me, the shameless man must have run his tongue over his drink-laced lips and mentally stripped me.

I detested the men in my world to the core, yet let them linger around me only because they were indispensable to my existence. I now wonder how I could have tolerated such open wantonness but that's what being a star is all about – being blasé, unabashed, and intrepid.

And then, there were the laymen in my world who whistled and frolicked as they watched me gyrate on the screen, fantasised limitlessly, and indulged in vicarious exploits that often reduced me to a mere symbol of pleasure than an entity with veritable emotions and a life of her own. To them, I was just a poster girl who anybody could make love to in thoughts.

At times I squirmed at such distasteful contemplation, but I drank it all in – the adulation, the flattery, and the sleaze of a world in which passing fancies reigned. Such was the glitz of the space that I dominated; such was its appeal. How was I to know then – when the world capitulated in front of me – that time would gradually pass and my prime would eventually pale? How was I to realise that memories of that delirious celebration of youth and renown is all that I would have to recount and take recourse to during the inevitable days of obscurity that lurked somewhere in the future? I was so young, so incorrigibly vain, and so foolishly unaware then.

Laxmibai hasn't turned up for three days now. The rains are to blame for it.

Streets have turned into streams of muddy water, carrying flotsam to unknown destinations. I can't see from the height of my home what kind of things floated and flowed, but the TV channels say there are human bodies and animal carcasses among other things. I flinch at the thought. The graphic details of the deluge below had made me turn the TV off.

I understand Laxmibai's difficulty and the reason for her absence, but it makes my musty living insufferable. She is my only immediate human connection to the world, my umbilical cord.

I have known Laxmibai since she was ten, when she used to tug along with her mother to work in my house. She was merely Laxmi then. She became a bai only when she took the place of her mother as our domestic help. This was soon after her mother had committed the most forgivable offense of stabbing Laxmi's father to death and then been sentenced to life imprisonment.

I don't describe the murder of her father as 'forgivable' for nothing. He was a man given to excessive drinking and beating of wife and children. The fact that he had a job in the mill did nothing to sober down his vicious temperament and vagrant ways. All it rather did was provide him with the additional wherewithal to make unholy liaison with women in brothels and other excesses to which Laxmi's mother was a mute, stoic witness.

And there were reasons for her silent suffering. The presence of a man in the house, albeit deviant and deceitful, provided ample protection to her three daughters from the preying eyes of men in the neighbourhood, most of who could turn into salivating beasts with uncontainable libido at the sight of a vulnerable feminine shadow lurking among them. Such unrestrained masculine nature made even an ill-tempered father acceptable to the girls who lurched between the provisional security that he provided and the lingering fear they had for him.

But one day when things came to a head, when in his drunken state he almost strangled his wife to death, she did the inevitable in self-defense. For the sake of the girls, as she said to the police and the court.

Laxmi and I secretly celebrated his death by sharing a chocolate after she enacted the grisly scene as though she were narrating a story from a cinema. As I could see, she had scant regard or affection for her father.

'Did your father beat you yesterday?' I remember asking Laxmi on several occasions when her mother came to work with bruises on her body.

'He does that most of the days,' Laxmi would say and flounce off into the garden dragging me along with her.

'My father never beats me,' I would say running along, more with relief than with a sense of pride. I could never come to terms with the thought of a father who found pleasure in thrashing his wife and children. It made me ask Laxmi questions of all kinds.

'What does he beat you for?'

'Anything,' Laxmi would still be unfazed.

'Anything?'

Laxmi would nod and curl her lips.

'But he buys us ice candy on some days,' She would add. It was as though the ice candy was reason enough for her to forgive his brutality. I admired the dispassion with which she accepted her life, with all its rough edges.

'Does your father beat you and Maaji?' she would ask, more to reiterate her notion about violent fathers than to pry.

I would merely shake my head, thinking and balking at the thought at the same time. Papa can never do anything that would make us sad and suffer, I would say.

'It can't be true. All fathers beat their children and their mother. It happens in all houses.' Laxmi was convinced of that. And then as an afterthought she added, 'And there is fighting too in all homes.'

'It isn't true. I have never seen Papa and Mama fighting,' I said categorically and smiled, recollecting the gentle kiss Papa placed on Mama's cheek and mine before leaving for the studios every day.

'That's because you are rich,' Laxmi declared, her voice lifting at the sudden thought and then dipping at the realisation of what it meant. 'Rich people are happy people. They don't cry, they don't have any trouble. They don't fight because they are happy.'

Laxmi made her thoughts known in a sudden burst of words that betrayed her envy.

'May be,' I said and smiled. This time I displayed a gentle air of pride that cast a gloom on Laxmi's face. I thought that her disappointment and envy were justified.

Happiness. Money. Love. Our home was lucky to have it all.

'My mother says not everyone can be rich.' Laxmi continued, 'But I hate to be poor. Is there some way your Papa can make us rich too?'

I shook my head. I didn't want to share any 'secret of richness' with Laxmi. It wasn't that I knew what made us rich and Laxmi poor, but I didn't want intruders in our happy world and so I said, 'Your mother is right. Not everyone can be rich and happy.'

I was glad that I didn't have to make Laxmi a part of this exclusive world. It was ours and I held it close to my heart.

I remember watching Laxmi with sympathy as she walked out of our house into the rain on that day, clutching her mother, the umbrella barely sheltering either of them. She deserved to be happy and rich, but I had no heart to share my special delights with her. She could have my old toys and clothes, she could be my playmate regardless of our differences, she could tell me ghost stories and get me shivering, she could tickle me to laughter, but she could never hope to be a part of my life.

Today, years later, lonely and wrecked by time's clueless ways, I wait impatiently for her to ring my doorbell. She is now more than a maidservant to me.

Taking Laxmi into my life was a decision I took years after that rainy day when I swore not to let anyone tread into our cozy life. But I think it was sometime during the course of the same year that the foundation for her to sneak into my life was laid. And I didn't notice it until much later. To be precise, until once, on my return home from the boarding school, I found Mama gone.

I was in my tenth grade then. I do not know what made Papa and Mama shunt me to a boarding school in the first place. The day they made the announcement I knew things were coming to an end, the happiness in my life was on a retreat, the love was taking leave, and the home that I never thought would betray me was beginning to distance itself from me.

'But why do I have to go?' I asked Mama.

'For your own good,' Was all she had to say. And as an afterthought, as though she had to give a more plausible explanation said, 'We want you to have a good education.'

'But I am already having it all good, am I not?' I persisted.

'We want it to be better. And you will not ask me any more questions. You will merely obey.'

I hadn't heard Mama talk to me like that ever before. Her tone wasn't menacing, but the firmness with which she said it was unpropitious. It was as though a shadow had fallen over our home: a shadow with horns and a spear in its hand. Little did I know that it would soon create a breach between Papa and Mama and that the growing distances would eventually rip the fabric of our family apart.

For the next three years Papa and Mama cleverly kept the secret of the rift and discontent in their marriage from me. They had decided that until I was old enough to understand and appreciate their incompatibility and maturely accept their parting ways as inevitable, they would put up the charade. It took a long time for me to realise that their relationship had been out of sync for a long time. They hadn't been much different from Laxmi's parents, except that the codes of civility and the pretensions of their social life didn't allow them to display it.

I am amazed that at no point did their conduct betray their smouldering relationship. They were a perfect couple who entered a gathering hand in hand, smiling and waving, a couple who defied showbiz norms and stayed married for more years than many of their contemporaries, a couple who the film world sighed over, and the flashlights gleamed on.

In the eyes of the world, it was the most endearing liaison until one day an unexpected spat at a party between them got reported in the gossip columns. Already weary of the long pretense, Papa and Mama ripped off the masks of their lives and announced that they weren't a couple anymore.

I felt deceived. I felt there was more honesty in Laxmi's family than mine. They at least fought and hated openly.

I wrote to them saying I was quitting studies and was going to take up work in the industry. I needed neither their support nor sympathy. I asked them to allow me to find my path on my own and not to fight a legal battle over my custody.

Mama initially wrote letters trying to say that it was inevitable, and I would understand someday but it didn't heal the bruise of their deceit in my heart. Papa on his part remained stoic, never once trying to clarify and for a long time I never knew why.

My reaction to my parents' separation might have appeared dramatic and rebellious, but it was irrepressible. It affected me more personally than it did them.

Being Papa's daughter and as young as sixteen, it wasn't difficult to find roles. I made a quiet beginning and slowly with a heady mixture of my sweltering youth and spirit of adventure, I scaled mercurial heights.

I was succeeding with a vengeance as though every rung on the ladder was an answer to Papa and Mama's act of dishonesty against me. I was so naïve to believe that proving my worth without their help was one way of getting back at them; a way of rejecting them so completely that it made snappy media reports that were aided by my brash statements against them.

I now look back at my ribald behaviour of those times with much repentance. It took a very long time for me to emerge from that state of loathing and affected sentiments.

'You needn't have made your life look like a celluloid drama,' I remember saying to Mama with contempt when we met at Papa's funeral fifteen years after they separated.

The words were pretentious, abrupt and inapt, both in terms of sense and situation, but they came on an impulse.

Mama looked at me and smiled, not wistfully, not arrogantly—just a smile that gave nothing away.

She had aged, but still carried that rare elegance that set her apart even in a crowd of mourners. I was impressed that she had made no effort to hide her age behind hair colour and make-up. She looked plain, both within and without. Her life seemed to carry none of the synthetic glitter of the film world. She seemed at peace with herself, and it amused me more than it irked.

Amusement soon turned to annoyance, and I spat out words that I had never imagined I would speak.

'Have you ever thought what it was like to find you gone one fine day? You left me with questions that I could ask no one, with an anger that till this day hasn't abated and a sense of betrayal that has preyed on me all these years.'

Mama watched me spew anger with the same tranquility that she maintained since the time she had arrived in the morning. She didn't weep for Papa, she didn't show an emotion. She merely seemed to complete a formality with her presence.

'I thought Papa and I were inseparable parts of your life. That was how we had lived, hadn't we? And after all those years of togetherness did you really have to leave? And I know it wasn't even for the love of another man.'

The sarcasm in my tone welled up and flowed over. I hadn't been able to ask her in all those years, but that day, it wasn't possible for me not to ask.

'It was your papa who didn't love us anymore,' Mama said gently. Her voice was devoid of reproach or regret.

'Impossible. I don't believe you'

Mama smiled again. This time a trace of disdain appeared on her face.

'You still love your papa very much,' she observed. 'But he had long since stopped loving us.'

And then Mama let the past scroll open, as though reading a movie script.

'Your papa was a great film maker, but he had his faults. Faults that I first refused to see, then overlooked, then put up with until one day my endurance gave way.'

I sat up and stiffened, baffled at what she revealed. I waited to hear more about the man I believed was grossly wronged by her.

'I had to leave without a word and without explanations. I couldn't have spoken about it to anyone then. I didn't want the world to know although it was the easiest thing for me to do to get even with him. It would have wrecked his career, but it would have had its effect on you too. His disrepute would have put your future in danger. You see, the film world is very whimsical and ruthless.'

I grew impatient.

'But Mama...'

Mama raised her hand as if to stop me from speaking.

'But today I can speak to you about it. I have no remorse and no fear.'

'Because Papa is no more? Because I have done well for myself?'

'No. Because... I can now look back at my past without regret. It is not significant anymore. When you can accept your past and talk about it without guilt or remorse only then do you become truly free in life. And I feel free. I am not attached to anything in my history. It gives me the strength to tell you that it wasn't me. It was your father, your papa.'

'What about him?'

'It was he who broke our home. And the world believed that it was I who walked out on him.'

'I still don't believe you.'

'I know you won't. And I don't insist you do, either. I have to tell you my truth to remove the stubs of my past from my life. I have to tell you for my sake... For me to be completely free.'

The evening air started getting cold. Mama pulled the saree over her shoulder and walked towards the garden chair beneath the guava tree. I followed her and sat across her, waiting for her to speak.

People, mostly celebrities from the film fraternity, were beginning to leave the bungalow and Mama watched them with indifference. She did not belong in their pack. She wasn't present at the funeral as Papa's ex-wife, and they acknowledged the fact only too well. No one came forth to offer condolences to her, although many people who knew her gave her a tentative nod of acquaintance when they crossed her path.

Papa had died leaving not many to earnestly mourn for him. It was a painful thought that made me swallow emptily.

The brief pause in our conversation made me restive. I wondered what was playing on Mama's mind; what did she feel if not regret, guilt and a sense of loss?

'You were telling me something,' I said, consciously avoiding addressing her as Mama.

'Sorry, I was distracted.'

She paused again, smiled at a passer-by, and asked, 'How many times have you fallen in love?'

It was an absurd thing to ask and I stared at her unable to respond.

'How is that relevant?' I asked after a few seconds.

'Love and money, though not always in that order, make things relevant or otherwise in this world. The two things that men and women fight and kill for, the two things that make countries war, the two things that make people strangers to themselves. The two most important things in life, according to most people in the world. If you don't have it, you suffer. If you have it in excess, you still suffer. The world seems to be divided into these segments of extremes. The secret of happiness lies in knowing the optimal level and staying there. The world would have been a much better place if only all men and women knew where to stop. Self-restraint—is the secret.'

Nervous and uncertain, I tried to think what Mama was up to. She seemed to drift into a mysterious realm that I was wary of stepping in. There was something blurred about her manner and I wished our conversation could end that very moment.

'I think I should be going. I have a photo shoot tomorrow,' I said rising to my feet.

'I thought you were eager to know what went wrong between us. I may never be able to tell you. This is our last chance at it. Take it or leave it.'

The casualness with which she said that baffled me. Didn't she say a little while ago that she needed to stub out her past completely by talking to me? Now she makes it sound as though the need was mine.

Why was I still standing there, I wondered.

I could merely have walked out of there without caring to answer. I had no obligation to help her clear her soul by listening to her past woes or whatever she chose to term them. I had nothing to offer her, neither love, nor pity, nor understanding. And it wasn't necessary for me to let her know about my private life. She had lost her moral right to it long ago. How many times have you been in love? How ridiculous of her to ask that of me!

But I stood on, unable to speak or move. I took long moments to reflect on what Mama's revelations meant to me. And then, I knew. I might not have cared to admit but the time had come for me to confront my past. And this woman, my mother, was giving me a chance to earn my freedom from my past. I had waited for it for years and now when it arrived, I am afraid of what secrets it might spill and I am trying to escape.

'Stay,' said my heart. 'Flee,' said my mind.

I felt a throb in my temple and I closed my eyes tight. Years of pain pressed against my nerves, and I sank into the chair.

'Tell me all that you have to say,' I whispered, my eyes still closed.

I felt Mama's hand on my arm. Suddenly, I wished I could fall in her lap and cry for all those years I had missed her in my life. I wished I could openly revile her for abandoning me and Papa. I wished I could tell her that I hated her so much only because as a child I had loved her so dearly.

'Do you hate me so much that you won't look at my face?' I heard her ask.

'I don't know,' I said opening my eyes and trying to fix my glance away from her.

'You are very beautiful, you've taken after your papa's features,' she observed and after a pause asked, 'Are you in love with someone?'

'Why do you ask?' I was irked again. But she didn't seem to care for the irritation that I so explicitly showed on my face.

'Because... love is the most natural feeling for a human being to have. And a pretty thing like you could not have escaped from its bounds. Not in the industry. It is a trade fair of love out there,' she said sarcastically. 'It could have only got worse with time. Relationships without scruples that thrive more on sex and scandal than connection with the soul, isn't that what love is all about in your industry?'

'You sound so banal and boring,' I wanted to say.

Instead, I said in a vexed accent, 'How can you speak like one of those common millions out there who think that the industry is a concourse of deceitful, sleazy men and women with no heart and soul and that they were born only to feed the common man's fantasies? You were a part of it too at some point of time.'

'But you know it is true, don't you? How many men and women are cheating on each other and blaming it all on the pressures of the new times? Can you say for certain that all those couples in your world who swear by their love will walk down the aisle eventually? And if they do whether they will stay put for the rest of their lives?'

'May be yes, may be no. But doesn't that possibility exist for those outside our world too? Why pick on us and what, for God's sake are we talking about? What has this got to do with whatever you wanted to tell me?'

Get the whole damn thing off your chest and get your freedom, and give me mine too, I wanted to scream.

'What I want to tell you has got everything to do with just that – love, morality, trust. Rather the lack of it. You are an idiot if you think the man who you are in love with has no fantasies about other women in the world. He has you beside him, he has another in his heart, yet another in his mind and yet another in his bed. That's what happened to me. And I wish it doesn't happen to you.'

Now, I was looking straight into Mama's face, but she had her gaze fixed on something behind me. Either on the Gulmohar in all its summer glory, or the vast expanse beyond.

'You don't mean to say Papa cheated on you? Did he have someone else in his life other than you? Was he in love with someone else in the industry?'

It wasn't impossible that a successful man like Papa could have liaisons outside home, but knowing him, it wasn't probable. I suspected that Mama was giving a new spin to the whole story about our past. She was portraying herself as a martyr by shoving a whole lot of grime on Papa, now dead and gone. What did she want from me?

'It wasn't about love at all, Seema,' she said in despair. 'He was a man with an insatiable appetite. At some point I had grown incapable of feeding his needs. So he made unaccountable relationships outside. Looking back I have wondered if he had always been an immoral drifter. I might have been too involved in our family to realise it, or I trusted him a lot because of the love we believed to have shared. So, the day I discovered that he slept with young female actors whom he gave a break, I knew I was married to the wrong man. When infidelity becomes a habit, the relationship becomes ugly and repulsive.'

I wanted to put a hand on her arm and tell her that I understood how it felt, but I desisted because thoughts about Papa could still not conjure up the image of an infidel man in my mind. I wonder what it is about fathers that make their daughters trust them so staunchly.

'And so you walked out?' I asked, having nothing else to say.

'No, I didn't. I stayed on, for your sake. Outside home we lived as a couple and inside, we were strangers. I allowed him all his indulgences for your sake.'

I didn't like the stress she gave to those words, for your sake. I felt she said it to stress that she had done me a favour for which she now expected me to be grateful.

'And when did the charade you put on for my sake end?' I asked impatiently.

'The day I saw Laxmibai with him.'

I put my hand to my mouth and gasped.

Now this was turning into stuff that films are made of. It sounded contrived and cunning on Mama's part to give such an unpalatable twist to her story. I got up to go, almost gagging on what I had just heard.

'Stop, you haven't heard it entirely,' she said gripping my wrist so hard that it hurt.

'I don't want to,' I said wrenching my hand free.

'You must know the full truth. You may believe it or not, but you must hear it from me. You can't go from here with spite in your heart for me.'

I stood on, unable to say anything.

Whatever Mama said in the next ten minutes punctured my ears, hammered my head, blighted my sight and pushed me back into the seat.

'It wasn't her fault really. She was pulled into it and then cornered. The money that he offered her did her in. She was in such dire condition that she could not refuse him. She found in it an easy way to escape the misery of poverty.

Do you know what she told me when I asked her about it? That she felt it was better than prostitution. She had no idea that that's exactly where it could have led her. Poor girl, your papa didn't spare even her for his needs and to think she was only a little over his daughter's age. Mama gently shuddered at the thought.

Poor girl. I wondered what made Mama so sympathetic towards Laxmibai. She did after all intrude into our life, I thought with disgust.

'That's their lot – immoral, opportunistic... And you talk of the industry?' I wanted to snap back. But I suppressed my urge to protest, as I spared a quick thought to the little girl who had always aspired to be rich and happy, like us. The girl who I never wanted to be a part of my life.

'Where is she now?'

'Who? Laxmi? She works at the home for the aged and school for the blind that I run in Delhi.'

Home for the aged and school for the blind? I look at Mama with intrigue. She was either a spotless Samaritan or a crafty charlatan. I struggled to assign her a definite designation.

'And Laxmi's daughter?'

'She is in a boarding school in Ooty. She is under my sponsorship.'

'Does Laxmi know where she is?'

Mama shook her head.

'For some reason I couldn't bear the thought of the child growing up in the squalor of the slums. She wasn't mine, alright, but she was your papa's. That way I felt responsible. It is odd to assume the responsibility of your husband's illegitimate child, but I could think of no other way then. The doctor said to Laxmi that her baby was still born. She mourned for days and then came to terms with it. It was

God's way of punishing her, she kept saying.'

The incredible revelations from Mama's past left me numb and speechless. One moment I felt heavy with muddled emotions and the other, I felt empty – completely devoid of thought.

Darkness and silence engulfed us as we sat reflecting in the twilight. It was home coming time for the birds that had their nests in the guava tree. Above us they chirped and screeched in glee. It sounded as though an entire community was in celebration of a reunion.

On the other side, the film world had packed up after the day's proceedings in Papa's house and the place wore a deserted look. There was no one in the bungalow except the two servants who had attended to Papa in his last days. Death had relieved Papa of his lonely, tarnished and pathetic existence, I thought with some satisfaction.

I didn't know where to place my sympathy – on Papa, Mama, Laxmi or her child, now somewhere away, lonely without either a father or mother. I imagined her solitude, her longing for a home and felt a sudden pang of sorrow.

'Now you may go. I want to sit here for some more time. I may never return to this place ever again,' Mama said. Her voice was wispy yet clear. She sounded like a woman rid of a lifetime's woes, privately relishing her moment of freedom.

'No, I want to be with you for a while,' I said, taking her hand and squeezing it. The deepening darkness made it difficult for me to catch the details of her face, but I knew she was smiling with satisfaction.

'But I have nothing more to say.'

'That doesn't matter. I just want to be with you for some more time,' I insisted.

Mama said nothing. Her silence made me uneasy. Now that the weight was off her chest, didn't she want me around her? I found myself fidgeting in the discomfort of the thought as moments passed by.

'I have had two heart breaks and one walk out. You had wanted to know,' I said suddenly.

'That wasn't important. I was merely asking.' She dismissed it lightly. I could see her silhouette in the light from the bungalow as she waved in the air.

'Presently there is no one in my life. I am sapped. I am in the process of scrubbing out the remains of my failed relationships and cleansing my soul,' I continued to say, not worrying if it interested her.

'I know. It happens,' she said without prying into details.

'Someday when I find someone who is worth the while, I will marry. I will let you know if I do.'

Mama nodded as if to merely acknowledge. I hoped she would say something; offer me solace, assurance and hope. Tell me that not all men were like Papa.

'Why didn't you marry again after separating from Papa? You could have easily found someone. You are a beautiful woman,' I asked, changing tack and trying to sound sprightly.

As I said that, I saw the glint in her eyes even in the diffused light that came from the bungalow.

'I could have found enough men for short-stinted affairs. And I don't deny that I found a few men attractive. But none caught my imagination enough to make a commitment. I did not want to have relationships based on sex alone. And in all these years, I haven't come across a man who would put companionship above physical desire.'

'It is still not extremely late. I would like it if you had someone in your life. It must have been a tough, loveless existence for you.'

'It hasn't been entirely loveless. I have had love from different quarters, but yes, they haven't been the kind of love that you are talking about. And now I have no stomach for that kind of love.

'How old are you now?'

'Fifty-five.'

'You look young for that age.'

'Does it matter?'

I merely shrugged in response.

'Mama,' I said and paused. I pulled my seat close to hers and said in a tremulous voice, 'I would like to see Laxmi and her daughter.'

'No, I don't think that would be a good thing to do. I don't want her to know anything about Shreya. She will not forgive me for lying and for keeping her daughter away from her, despite the good things I have done.'

I hung my head in disappointment and sighed. The fact that her secret still bothered her made me wonder if she was truly free from the ghosts of her past. I thought of the nature of things bygone and how they kept coming back in different forms to haunt and hassle human beings. Now, here, strangely it was in my form.

'You can trust me to keep your secret. I have nothing to gain by telling anyone anything,' I said categorically and took her hands in mine.

She nodded as if to acknowledge my promise and became contemplative.

'Secrets are such burdens in life, aren't they, and yet so inherent to human nature. Who on earth has lived without a secret sagging in his heart?' I said breaking the silence. It was more a loud thought than a statement.

'The world is livable today only because there is a little bit of mystery in everyone's life. If all men and women were to lay bare their secrets, life would become a torture. Love and peace would be wiped out forever. Lies are essential and inevitable,' Mama said taking her hands off mine and rising to go.

'You didn't tell me. Will you take me to Laxmi and her daughter?'

'Yes, I will.'

As we walked toward the bungalow in silence, Papa's lawyer came up to me. He did not acknowledge Mama's presence beside me and she didn't seem to mind.

'I have asked the servants to pack up and leave. You can lock the house and keep the keys with you. I will inform you when the notice from the court arrives. Should you need any assistance, call me.'

'Papa had pledged the bungalow,' I said to Mama as soon as the lawyer left. 'He led a wayward life. Was it because we deserted him? Or was he wild and reckless by nature?'

Mama chose not to reply. She reached into her handbag and fished out an airline boarding pass, on the back of which she scribbled her telephone number and handed it to me.

'Mama, don't you mourn his death?' I asked taking the number, eager to evoke in her one last flicker of emotion for Papa.

'No, I don't,' she whispered firmly and turned to go.

There was no defiance in her manner, only a hint of the hurt that Papa had handed her and the pain that she had carried in her heart all those years. As I watched her walking away, I felt a sudden longing.

'Mama,' I called from behind her and paced up. 'Mama, can I hug you?'

Before I realized it, I was in her arms. Silently we wept in the darkness for all our spoken and unspoken sorrows. Like a mother and a daughter. Nothing could have taken away from the magic of that surreal moment. It was our true moment of redemption.

It has taken nearly a week for the telephone department to restore the phone lines that went kaput during the rains. The rain Gods have been sober for the past ten days and it is a relief to have the sun beam in through the window although the air is still sultry and uncomfortable.

'Did Shreya baby call, chotimem?' Laxmibai asks over her shoulder as she wipes the windowpane.

Laxmibai has come after a gap of ten days and her presence and chatter fill the empty spaces in the house. Every day she brings in stories and gossip of all kinds from her colony – marriages, deaths, elopements, affairs, brawls and everything possibly inconsequential to me. But I let her talk and purge her heart. I believe that I owe this much to her for the favours she has done to me, some knowingly and some unknowingly.

'No, the telephone was down for over a week. She might have tried calling,' I say, hoping that Shreya would soon call.

'When will she come with the children? I am longing to see them.'

'Oh, I don't know. She says it is difficult to fly such long hours with Bittubaba and the little baby. And I agree. She would rather wait for the baby to be at least two before she travels.'

'That's at least another year or so away,' Laxmibai says with disappointment. I draw my lips and arch my brows as if to endorse her sense of regret.

'She now wants me to go to her. Isn't that foolish of her to ask me? I keep saying that I can't sit on an eighteen-hour flight either. And tell me Laxmi, how is it possible for me to go out into the world after all these years?'

'Why not mem? You have merely chosen to close yourself to the world. It isn't so bad outside yet. I don't know why you have to live like this. Who will look after you if something were to happen to me?' Laxmi says dropping the wipe and squatting on the floor, as if vexed with my condition.

I look at Laxmi with amazement and a secret admiration. The dreamy eyed woman who was abused by her father in childhood, who was used and dumped in her youth by a rich man, the woman who tossed her life for the sake of her siblings who gave her nothing in return in her old age, the woman who has seen all the profanity and betrayals, was calling the world 'not so bad yet'. I smile feebly at her desperate but wasted attempt to kindle my wilted spirits.

'I am tired with the world, Laxmi. That's the reason. There is nothing out there that I want to know, see or experience. I have done it all. I am at peace with myself and I don't need too many people in my life. I am better off without them.'

'You are lucky to be able to accept everything in life, mem. I wish I could be like you,' she says, missing the tedium with which I spoke those words.

I see a shadow of regret saunter across her forlorn face. I am amused that she has always wanted to be in my shoes. I wonder what it is that makes her think that I was and am still a happy person despite every deprivation that exists in my life. I am unmarried and have no family, I have no friends or social engagements, and my only relation Shreya lives in another continent. There is nothing enviable about my life today.

I watch Laxmi as she rises from the floor with some effort and begins to dust the photo frames hung on the wall. Her eyes linger on a family photograph of Shreya, her husband Ryan and their children Roshan and Lisa for a while before she takes it off the hook and wipes. I wonder what thoughts are swirling in her mind.

The weight of a secret unnerves me every time she talks about Shreya. I have always wanted to deter her from talking about Shreya, but I have no way of telling her so. I feel miserably incapable of keeping the subject of Shreya forbidden to Laxmi even as it makes me panic time and again. It is as if talking about Shreya would expose the truth to Laxmi and Shreya would be gone forever from my life. The insecurity surges and emerges in a torrent of words.

'Why do you have to take it in your hand to wipe it, Laxmi. What if you drop it? Haven't I told you many times?' I say suddenly. The rage rattles my body and I sink into the sofa.

Laxmi seems oblivious to the yelling. She has probably come to accept my sudden bouts of temper as the natural, irreparable aspect of an aging, lonely, one-time star whom the world has forgotten. Oddly, she takes pride in the fact that she is my only close relation in the world apart from Shreya and her family that barely relates with me. It makes her accept my deficiencies without malice.

The seething moment is past and I return to a state of induced tranquility.

With Mama too gone, there is no one to put the secret of my life in jeopardy. There is no one who can take Shreya away from me. She is and will be my adopted daughter, a gift from Mama for life.

Laxmi puts the photograph back on the wall, gently wipes it with the end of her saree, then turns to me and says, 'If nothing, you have Shreya baby to call your own. You are lucky.'

'Yes, I am,' I say, rising to my feet and turning away from her, choking on a tide of emotions that threaten to spill over. 'I have always been lucky, as you say.'

Behind me I hear Laxmi speaking, but I don't pay attention. I find myself caught in a whirlpool of thoughts from the past and the present and feel like a carcass in the flood waters – lifeless and swept away.

CHAPTER TWO

A Gift for Mangalam

Selvan walked into the City Centre Mall inhaling the fragrance so typical of malls in the city. He greedily took in the air filled with the scent of opulence, of Arabian and French perfumes, from the fabric of rich shoppers. He gazed at the stores with their dazzling spotlights under which things beyond his means lounged in anticipation, people who breezed in with credit cards and walked out with carts of wares, men and women whose attire and attitude evoked constant amusement and wonder in Selvan.

The mall was Selvan's favourite weekend haunt. There was something about it that seized his laboured soul and senses and provided something unique and refreshing to his spirits. On Fridays, he would don his best set of clothes, spray Brut under his arms, smear an after-shave on his closely shaved chin, and share a taxi with men, most of who, like him, had no specific purpose to go to the mall except to witness, many times with spite, the celebration of life by richer human beings.

There he would merge with the crowd, feeling one with its many splendours, wonder at people's odd needs and tastes in life, study their curious aspects, delight in the parade of beautiful women who thought nothing of baring their shoulders and hips, and when his soul sagged with the satisfaction of having seen it all, he would lumber out into the hot, humid air outside.

Nothing ever compared to the mall experience to Selvan, not even a round of rummy with friends or a breezy seaside stroll. The City Centre was where all his dreams culminated. It was where his hopes came to roost.

Selvan had visited the mall numerous times yet had not spent money on anything that it so proudly paraded. He had never lost sight of the fact that most things were beyond his means, and he was content to watch them from a distance, like one watches museum exhibit. There were times when he had felt a longing to walk into the stores, ask the prim salesgirl to show him a few things, consider them with the secret eyes of an admirer and ultimately return them pretending to be unimpressed – didn't like the colour or the design.

But he could never push himself into such sham; he feared that his manner and his form could easily give him away. The salesgirl would see through the falsehood, she would smell the odour of hard toil, the squalor of his work and the hollowness of his pursuit. She would suppress a sneer and walk away leaving Selvan to melt in dismay.

But this time there was a definite purpose to his going to the mall. He had marched into its portals with the poise of a serious buyer. He had a wallet that had finally found its significance and was bursting with money; it was now secretly basking in its newfound worth. It is a different matter that it was the weight of borrowed money. But money is money and Selvan had gathered all his resources to make his first purchase at the Mall.

Actually, he wasn't the kind of man who borrowed money. He was content to live within his means. He ate what he cooked in his small labour cabin, wore what was sold in the bargain stores, played cards only in the first week of the month when he had some money to wager, and made phone calls to his hometown only once in two or three months. But this time it was different.

He was going home and he had to borrow to buy gifts for his family. People in his circuit generally helped each other in matters like this. Going home on vacation was a big event and the period that preceded their departure was a frenzied one – scrimping their money, finding lenders, planning gifts, buying them and finally stacking them in cardboard cartons. The delight of going home was unsurpassed and they revelled in it till they returned to face the loans that they took months thereafter to repay. Sometimes it even extended up to their next vacation when they would launch themselves into a borrowing spree all over again. It was a routine among the men of his kind. They lived within a constant spiral of lending, borrowing, and repaying.

Selvan had arranged a neat sum for his first visit home in four years. He first made a list of the people he would have to buy presents for. His mother, sisters, brothers and their spouses, cousins and finally, his wife, Mangalam.

Mangalam always figured at the end of the list, not because she was insignificant, but she was the newest one on the list. She was the most recent addition to his domestic circle, which was an amalgam of near and distant relations. Buying gifts for the demanding posse was a thankless task. He had to match people with the presents or there would be complaints. He had to be impartial and generous or there would be complaints. He had to remember the remotest link or there would be complaints.

It was the way families responded to men in the yonder who came once in a few years with bags full of gifts. There were expectations that were only half met, there were desires that were only partially fulfilled, there were hopes that fell limping before they were even realised. It held true for all of them — the men, and the families. Yet, they all looked forward to the once-in-many-years celebration of giving and gifting, meeting and merry making. And the air of grouse and nitpicking that descended soon after the gift cartons opened eventually dissipated and a general bonhomie prevailed until the end of the vacation.

The first vacation home after marriage was marked by an acute distress. Selvan clearly remembered Mangalam's teary-eyed complaint that he had no love for her anymore. She had said it so suddenly and with such unprecedented conviction that Selvan's heart punctured and fell flaccid in front of her.

He did not love her anymore, she declared categorically. By love she meant 'special love', the love a man has for his wife. Rather she was to him just like any other member in his large family that lived under one roof to share everything from food to clothes, people and even their affection and hatred.

'Why would you consider me special? I am just one among the crowd,' she said a day after he landed on his vacation.

Her manner wasn't as annoying as it was intriguing or even charming. She was not loud and melodramatic like the other women in the family. She was solemn and sedate in her manner of making her protestation. Her voice wavered between a whisper and a string of gasps. It was as though she could break into a sob at any moment, but held her tears back within the margins of her kohl-lined eyes.

She rolled her saree around her finger, dropped her chin, and made such a picture of disenchantment that it broke Selvan's heart. It pained to hear her speak things he had never imagined. How could she say that he didn't love her anymore? That he hadn't even loved her enough in the four years of their marriage. How could it come to such an abrupt end as she suggested?

But Mangalam had her reasons.

'You never thought of me when you were away. If you had, would you buy me just the same things that you have bought for your sisters and others? I am just one among the big army of people in this house. Do you know that I got the leftovers of the things you brought? The saree that no one chose, the perfume that all had sprayed and tested, the powder that your sister-in-law thrust into my hands after making her choice first...You never got me anything special. After all these years of waiting, all that I get is the scrap, the tidbits.'

Kohl-lined tears began to trickle down and Mangalam made no effort to wipe them off.

'I had thought that you would have tucked something special in your bag for me. Something that no one else got. A surprise,' she muttered.

Selvan wondered what it was that she had expected. Something special, a surprise... he tried to think.

Finding no means to assuage his wife, he took her hand into his and said, 'You have my love, very special love that no one else has.'

Mangalam shook her head. She meant that there was no special love, only a common, shared love, like a common, shared meal.

'Special love means buying special things, taking me to Ooty, buying me jasmine strands, singing praises of my beauty. We can at least go to the beach and sit while holding hands, shooing the intrusive peanut vendors away and watching the sunset while I run my hands through your hair.' Mangalam gazed past her husband, her moist eyes glistening at the prospect of a beach side romance, and a smile beginning to break on her lips.

Selvan watched Mangalam's animated description of love with a sense of awe and surprise. Did she watch too many movies while he was away? She had acquired such odd and fanciful perceptions about love, expecting him to do things he had never thought possible amidst the vast, compelling presence of his family. He could never imagine taking Mangalam to Ooty or to the beach without being escorted. Nor did he have the nerve to do it on the sly. He could not buy jasmine for her without buying it for his sisters. They and his mother had always staked their claim to his affections more vociferously, reminding him time and again that they were his own blood. They stopped short of saying that his wife was not his own blood and hence deserved only a small portion of his life. For the same reason they believed that Selvan would never put anyone, not even his wife before them.

As for singing praises of Mangalam's beauty, Selvan thought it was too theatrical an act to perform even in the private hours at night.

'Okay if not singing, then at least a special gift. You could have done that. It is only because you don't love me any more than you love the others.'

'Okay, I will buy you something special. What do you want?'

'No, it is okay. I had wanted it from there. Not from here and certainly not after my asking for it.'

Mangalam struggled to convey her thoughts to her husband. That it was the excitement of finding in his bag a token of his special love for her that she had wanted to experience. That it was the feeling of being someone special to him that she looked for, that it was the pride of being the wife of the man who earned in thousands that she enjoyed. That she considered their love, no matter how much distanced by time and space, was unique and irreplaceable, and how much she yearned to be reassured that he loved her more than anyone or anything else in the world.

❧❧❧

Selvan wanted to make no such mistake this time. He consciously put Mangalam on top of his list and spent days thinking of a special gift. It had to be unique. It had to be something that he would not buy for anyone else. It had to profess his undying love for her. And for once, the price didn't matter. He could mortgage his entire life for this one special gift.

'A diamond ring...' suggested his friend, Vasu.

'It is special, but not special enough,' said Selvan scratching his head. He knew that a ring whether with a diamond or any other gem is just another piece of ornament and it would be nothing special for Mangalam. She had no fondness for jewellery.

No, not an ornament, he decided.

'What else for a woman other than clothes and jewellery?' wondered Vasu.

In the following days, his friends came up with suggestions that varied from the most mundane to the most bizarre. They made suggestions with their respective wives in mind and the kind of things they came up with made for moments of laughter, embarrassment, and ridicule. The trouble with their ideas was that they lacked originality. None of them could think beyond electronic and kitchen items, nail polishes and perfumes. When someone suggested a multi-purpose mixer, Selvan imagined his mother lunge at it even before poor Mangalam got her hands on it. Anything that got a parking space in the kitchen would become common property. The fate of a tape recorder or a Walkman would be the same – found, fought over, and claimed by the more gregarious members of his family.

'I want some suggestion for a gift for my wife and not advice on how to reset our lives,' said Selvan to Murugappan, who was still busy thinking against the evening sea breeze that brought along with it the wetness of a humid summer. He had his eyes turned up to the sky, his mouth slightly open, and his index finger gently tapping his lower lip in deep contemplation. He then curled his lips and shook his head in defeat.

'No, I can't think of anything. Thank God I am not married.'

'You will, sooner or later and then you would know.'

'I will lay down conditions first. No demands for a special gift.'

Selvan laughed at the prospect.

'Actually there is no such thing as a special gift in this world,' declared Murugappan philosophically, rising to his feet and dusting the beach sand off his pants. 'It is what each one of us considers special that makes it special.'

Selvan nodded and agreed contemplatively. He wondered what had inspired Murugappan to pronounce something so sublime and sensible. It could have been the sea, the breeze, or the setting sun. He rose, picking his slippers and began to walk, scuffing the sand up. The sand felt soft under his work boot ravaged feet.

'I think I know what to do,' he said, more to himself than to Murugappan.

☙☙☙

Selvan decided that he would make the purchase from The Mall. He would spend time walking around the stores that blinked under their spotlights and assess what could possibly make for a special gift; something that he would buy for no one else except Mangalam. He would know it as soon as he set his eyes on it. His heart would send signals, like it does in matters of love...and marriage.

He remembered how after spending two vacations viewing girls and rejecting them for a variety of reasons, his heart had approved Mangalam the very moment he saw her. He knew that she was the one for him from the moment she walked in to serve him and his brothers, coffee and snacks. He had set his heart on her despite her squint and her reed thin frame that seemed so fragile that his brothers teased him in turns.

'If you are not careful, you would have a pile of crushed bones in your hands every morning.'

'And then she would make a perfect rattle toy for you to play with,' said another.

It took no time for Selvan to be convinced that she was good looking, at least when compared to him. She was certainly a windfall to someone whose naturally dark skin was further charred by the desert sun and who had not even in his dreams expected to marry someone with such a glowing complexion as Mangalam's. She was a once-in-a-lifetime discovery. A God send. And he took secret delight in the jealousy that his not-so-good looking sisters-in-law harboured towards him and his wife and sometimes even wondered what could have made her settle for him after all. She could certainly have found someone more handsome. He never ventured to ask her the loaded question. It was sufficient that she had chosen him over all the men in the world. He was immensely satisfied with the thought that his children would acquire Mangalam's good looks, sans the squint.

But that was before the doctor had made the accursed pronouncement that they will not have babies. From then on, she was his only child, and he had sworn to himself to indulge her every whim and wish, more in a manner that a doting parent does to a precocious child than to compensate for the imperfection in their lives.

So whenever she accused him of not loving her any more than his family, he felt crestfallen. And that was why he had felt compelled to buy her a special gift this time. It was the only way he could make her believe that she was priceless to him. Her demand was after all, so childlike.

Being Friday, the mall was substantially crowded. Selvan stood at the centre of the giant structure, luxuriating in the air-conditioned, opulent interiors and appraising the outlets around that sold expensive garments, jewellery, watches, perfumes, artifacts, cosmetics, optical lenses, and sunglasses. He considered each of them, walking towards the entrance, taking a quick peek and scurrying away before being accosted by the saleswoman. Spoilt for choice, he walked to the centre of the mall again. He stood watching the fountain, thinking. He wondered how it was that people around him knew what exactly to buy and where to find it. He read his wristwatch like people seized by restiveness generally did: not to know the hour, but just to let the chaos in his mind ease and cool off.

Across him, the mannequins in the apparel store showed off their newest wear, clinging passionately to their lifeless, yet sophisticated figure – the contours of their body accentuating the charm of the apparel that swaddled them; the plunging neckline briefly catching the eyes of passers-by. Not the kind of clothes that Mangalam would wear, he thought. She had never worn anything apart from sarees. Not even the ubiquitous Indian salwar kameez.

'I have never worn modern clothes,' she said when Selvan first suggested that she wear salwar kameez. 'It makes me feel odd, especially in front of your brothers.'

To Mangalam, any attire other than saree was immodest. It was compulsory to have the six yards around her modesty.

'You are of such small frame that it will not look indecent,' said Selvan, referring to her small breasts and slender hips with a swift wave along her contour.

Mangalam was quick to take exception to his remark; she never found comments of such kind palatable and duly protested any sexual allusions. According to her they were indecent too and hence a strict taboo.

'Won't you ever change? Speaking such things!' she showed displeasure with a lovable grimace that disappeared as quickly as it had appeared.

Selvan ascribed her beliefs more to her innocence and lack of understanding about the ways of the modern world than to anything more sinister. His absence from home only made her more sensitive to such issues and the constant presence of his brothers making her deeply conscious and circumspect. She was a romantic at heart, longing for Selvan to arrive and express his love in ways that initially baffled him – gifts, jasmine, and outings – yet she was archaic in many other ways. The spate of movies that she watched in the home video did nothing to change her beliefs and manner. She picked up the far-fetched, make-believe aspects of the movies than the real. She was credulous and cagey and this made her increasingly endearing to Selvan.

Sometime later – after dozens of people went past him – Selvan drifted into the garment store, still caught up in his thoughts. He wafted in like a feather, thinking about Mangalam, without stopping at the gates to ogle at the mannequins. Columns and columns of clothing greeted him from their hangers and Selvan felt marooned in a sea of unfamiliarity. He wondered what it was that he had stepped into the store for: to make a purchase, to look around the sights or to merely make a spectacle of himself.

'Can I help you, Sir?'

Selvan was pleasantly surprised to be addressed with such reverence, another first in his life. For several moments after that, he shunned thoughts about the class that he belonged to – a manual worker who accompanied the sewage tankers and prior to that for years, a lawn mower in the city's vast landscape – and took on the pride of being a shopper in a high-end store in the mall and basked in it. He was grateful to the young, thin, dolled-up saleswoman for the rare honour. He felt pleased that she did not see through his mediocrity and even if she had, she did not make an issue about it.

'Can I help you?' she heard him repeat. He felt a trifle disappointed that she had chosen to drop the 'Sir' and his heart sank beneath the waves of multi-coloured attires around him. But it had felt good, even if it was only for once. He felt the strange bearing the money in his pocket had on the woman and thought smugly about the honour that it brought to a man.

'I am....I am just looking around,' he said haltingly.

The woman nodded, smiled tightly and waited as Selvan paced through the warren of clothes, with trepidation, jabbing and sliding the hangers aimlessly. What had he walked into the store for?

'Are you looking for children's wear?'

Ugh! Why can't she leave me to myself? Selvan wondered and then realising that he was in the children's section where little frocks with frills and laces played merry go around, said, 'Yes...children's too. But first I need something for...' he took a quick breath and said quickly, '...my wife.'

He looked bashful, without actually meaning to.

The woman smiled and duly led him to the ladies section. Selvan felt vexed to walk through the labyrinth that displayed ladies' wear and became aware of the futility of his long winding tour behind the saleswoman. Mangalam would never wear anything of this kind, he concluded. Then what on earth was he doing there, senselessly following a petite woman who did not have the slightest notion of his wife, her manner and her preferences?

Selvan turned around and considered the distance to the exit. Could he dart across and make an escape? But he knew the pitfalls of such an escapade; he could be taken for a shoplifter and be chased until they discovered that he was just another aspiring shopper with limited means. It could unmask him and his status would be revealed for all to know turning the mall that he so hankered after, his ultimate nemesis.

The disrepute that he would be laden with made him follow the narrow path.

'Skirts and blouses, Trousers...?

'I am not sure. Can I see on my own?' It almost meant, please, could you leave me alone? I am sick of being guided through. And I don't need your help, in any case.

'Of course. You can call me if you need help.'

Selvan nodded desultorily. He took a deep breath as the woman withdrew and disappeared into her territory of sorting and arranging apparels tried and rejected by customers. It was as though she had given up on him as a prospective customer, for she did not materialise ever again into his view. Nor did he seek her out.

But something stranger and more unexpected happened in the next half an hour. As soon as the saleswoman left, Selvan closed his eyes, thought of Mangalam, and turned a full circle. And like a blind man, felt the air in front of him and took a few wavering steps forward. He was surprised not to bump into anything on his way. It was as though the sea of apparel in front of him had willingly parted to make way for him. He took another full turn and opened his eyes. What he saw in front of him overwhelmed him.

He stood awestruck in front of the lingerie corner. He gave the arena a quick sweeping glance and unable to resist the temptation, stepped into the territory of bras, under pants, nightdresses, swimsuits, and other hard to define feminine clothing.

With a heart pounding heavily against his chest more out of anxiety than out of stimulation, Selvan sailed amidst the most intimate possessions in a woman's wardrobe, apprehensive to feel them, glancing sideways to make sure that he wasn't being watched, and amused by the grandeur and exclusivity of the things that women like Mangalam, his sisters, mothers, sisters–in–law and others in the neighbourhood attached so little importance to. To them they were just accessories devoid of splendour, things forced by their womanly needs, they could not forego and so they continued wearing them, day after day, even long after they were stretched and worn. The cloth line in the house bore their burden just as stoically as the women did. The pattern and design inconsequential in their domestic scheme of things.

But not anymore, Selvan decided; at least for Mangalam. She would now have a designer set that would give her femininity a charitable amount of pride and respect. There was no doubt that the other women in the family would be appalled by the brazenness and even be envious of her new possessions, but Selvan couldn't care less. He had found his special gift for her; so personal, so romantic and so very special. And this time he would certainly take her on a trip to Ooty, he decided.

All the while, he was conscious that Mangalam could be scandalised by his choice and there was every chance of her picking up a private row with him. But Selvan knew ways to get around her. He was an astute husband and lover, and knew methods to disarm and enchant his irate wife.

'I didn't mean anything like this when I asked you for a special gift. How could you be so shameless?' she would demand. And as though waiting for cue, tears would stream down at her first utterance.

He would look into her eyes, take her in his arms, and hold her tight as she tried to wriggle out, and serve heart-wrenching questions, intoned melodramatically.

'What is shameless about this? Am I not your husband, someone who shares your life's smallest and biggest things? Do you have to be so orthodox? Do you still consider me an outsider? Don't you see the love that I have put into this gift? All right, if you so hate it, I will throw it out. Or burn it.' And so on. He would temper her down to cloying levels of intimacy and eventually make her accept the gift.

The thoughts regaled him as he began his search for the perfect set of lingerie for Mangalam. He held her in his mind and matched sets with her image – size, colour, and pattern. He thought of Baywatch when he saw the tantalising swimsuits lined up and for a moment wished he could take Mangalam to the beaches in Goa.

Goa was a long shot considering that even a trip to Ooty with her would warrant clever planning, complete secrecy, and crafty execution. Otherwise, he would have the entire family in tow, making a thorough washout of the romantic endeavour. So, he left the swimsuits in their racks and settled for more viable options, for there was no scope for too much adventure in his life. There could be no beaches and Baywatch in his life, not with his large family around.

Within half an hour he emerged at the billing counter, feeling utterly self-conscious about his purchase. He was pleased that the lady at the counter took no notice of it, nor did she express surprise or shock at his choice of wares from the store. A smile and a courteous 'thank you' at the end of the business were all that she had to offer and Selvan hurried out of the store, glad that the ordeal was over. He felt a renewed surge of pride at finally having made a purchase from the Mall and he cruised out, gently swinging the shopping bag in his hand and producing a soft, impish smile on his lips at the thought of presenting the gift to Mangalam.

He wished he could get on a plane and reach her in the next few hours or if possible, the very next minute. It was getting difficult to contain his sense of exhilaration, but sadly, there were two more weeks to go (during which time he would have to shop for the rest of the family) before he could do that and until then, the gift would lay nestled in his air bag, waiting just as he would to land at its due destination.

On the day of his arrival, the family waited at the airport braving the scorching summer. The women folk and children dressed garishly as though there was a wedding party to attend and the men –Selvan's two brothers – in trousers and full sleeve shirts buttoned at the wrists.

If they didn't make a quaint spectacle, it was mainly because there were many such families waiting animatedly at the gates, to catch the first glimpse of their foreign returned relative, to hold his hand, to steal his glance, to embrace, to capture his gift laden bags and to make him the sole focus of their lives for the next few weeks. It is commonplace to find swarms of people at the arrival and departure gates every day of the year, the former gushing with the excitement of receiving a relative unmet for long and the latter tearfully watching the men go away, disappear deep inside the airport terminal.

'Can't wait it seems,' said a sister poking a finger at Mangalam. Mangalam merely smiled although it was true that she had barely slept in the days ahead of Selvan's arrival, spending nights thinking, wondering, waiting with a clamorous heart. She knew that there would once again be a battle of claims to Selvan's attention and affection within the family, and she was the weakest contender among all in the house. And how much she hated her in-laws for depriving her of her husband's exclusive love for her!

And now this teasing by them, she thought with disgust. But she continued to smile, lest Selvan should come out and find her frowning, downcast and unappealing. She was certain that on coming out Selvan would first strive to find her face from among the simmering cluster on the other side of the railing. The thought made her smile faintly behind the kerchief she held to her mouth.

'I will sit next to him in the van,' said a niece in her new, but over-sized frock.

'No, I will,' said her brother, only a couple of years older.

'No, I will,' squeaked yet another nephew of Selvan.

And then the brawl between the five little contenders began. Mangalam watched without endeavouring to calm them, throwing exasperated looks at them and secretly detesting the contest for Selvan.

'None of you will. Only the elders will sit next to him,' said a sister-in-law referring to Selvan's brothers. 'The children will sit in the front next to the driver.'

That was incentive enough to calm the children.

Selvan was going home after four years and he spent the seemingly interminable journey through the air turbulence and air-hostess courtesies wondering what changes time could have wrought on the people and places that he would soon go to. How much more would his mother have aged, how fatter his brothers and brothers-in-law would have grown, how much more garrulous his sisters would have become, how much more docile or dreamy-eyed Mangalam would have turned, how much would have the kids in the house grown.

Each vacation was a rediscovery of his family, everyone coming across so differently each time as though they had been through a continuous process of change in his absence. He wondered if it was his own perception of them that changed every time; if the distance between them had distorted their impressions in his mind so much that when he met them after four years, he saw them in a new light.

He walked out of the immigration area with bated breath, unsure of what to expect. He did not want to think. He rolled the trolley filled with his family's expectations towards the exit door. And then he saw them, all of them at once. His family. He saw the exhaustion on their faces brought by the heat and the waiting being overshot by the thrill of seeing him walk towards them.

'Ey, Selva...' His brothers took him in an embrace before taking over the trolley. His sisters came to hold his hands and the children tugged at his shirt.

And then, Mangalam.

He saw her waiting for him to go to her, without taking precedence to receive him. She knew that he would go up to her first and so she waited behind the crowd.

So much like herself, thought Selvan. He went towards her, unmindful of his brothers' animated queries, holding her in sight and considering her intently.

'Hey, you have grown fat,' he said instantly, resisting his instinct to take her into his arms or at least to hold her hands. It wasn't the done thing in the presence of people.

Mangalam nodded coyly.

'And you have become darker and leaner,' she whispered.

He wondered if she was disappointed that it was so. At the same moment, her unexpected expansion from a bony young thing to a rotund shaped woman made his heart sink.

How and when did she gain so much weight, he wondered. He thought of the special gift as he walked with her to join the rest of the family. There were slim chances of it fitting her now.

'How did you grow so fat?' he asked her softly pressing her arm inside the van during their ride home.

'I am not so fat,' Mangalam protested.

Selvan knew it was true. She wasn't too fat, but she was fat for the special gift. She cannot squeeze into it by any means and the thought frustrated him.

'But you were nice when you were thin,' he said struggling to conceal his disappointment over her sudden growth in size.

'So you don't like me now?'

'I didn't mean that.'

'Then?'

'I just said you were better then.'

'People say it is only now that I have begun to look mature like a married woman,' she said proudly.

Selvan couldn't deny that. She had acquired a complete and complimentary look, but what of the gift that he had so painstakingly chosen for her and so eagerly brought with plans of a trip to Ooty, where she would wear it for his eyes only?

He perfunctorily answered the questions that were flung at him from various sides of the van. He nodded in between, shook his head, stared out the window, smiled, and spoke in monosyllables.

Tired from the initial chatter and amusement, the family began to snooze during the two-hour drive home.

'What have you brought for me?' asked Mangalam, tugging at Selvan's sleeve. Her voice was barely audible, as though she was trying to wangle out secret information from him.

'There is something,' said Selvan with a contrived smile.

He couldn't lie and so he ducked Mangalam's probing questions with stealthy replies.

'What is it?' Mangalam's eyes opened wide with curiosity. Her child like delight moved Selvan as he took her hand into his.

'Can't tell you now. It is a surprise.'

'Special?'

'Very special.'

Mangalam moved closer to Selvan, put her head on his shoulder, and slowly drifted into sleep. Selvan looked at her sympathetically and simpered at the irony. Of what use was the gift to her now? It would be such a travesty to give it to her, something so special, yet so ineffective.

With each passing day and changing excuses from Selvan, Mangalam's curiosity began to pale into wariness and then to disappointment and resignation.

'You are lying. You haven't brought anything for me. It is okay if there is nothing, but it is better to let me know. At least, I wouldn't keep waiting,' she said, hoping she would be proved wrong, for once.

For some reason she was convinced that Selvan could not have disregarded her so blatantly, despite the overpowering bond he had with his family. It wasn't right to suspect his love, she thought with tender consideration.

'Believe me, there is something for you. But you can't have it now. I will give it to you at the appropriate moment. I want you to believe me.'

At that point she saw the earnestness in his eyes and something changed within her. She then wanted to tell him that it really didn't matter. It was enough if he loved her, the gift was only a symbol and what a fool she was to attach so much importance to a present! But she did not speak; she just looked into his eyes, soaking in that moment of realisation.

As days fell by, Mangalam forgot all about the gift, the residue of hope fading into the energised atmosphere of the house in the wake of Selvan's arrival – the trips with him and the family, the joint conversations, her involvement in the cooking of special dishes for him, and the private nights in their room.

Selvan however found it hard to conceal his disappointment and returned time and again to the gift that he had so carefully concealed from Mangalam's eyes. He opened the plastic shopping bag from a corner and peeked inside as though he was peeking into another man's house through the window and put it back with a deep, chagrined sigh. It disturbed him that Mangalam did not ask for it since. He felt as if her disinterest had robbed the gift of its appeal and worth, and that it did not matter anymore, either to him or to her.

Selvan marvelled at her transient nature, so insistent at one point, and so unconcerned and blithe now. She had very small desires and dreams which she could concede as easily as she created. She could understand as easily as she could misunderstand. She could accept conditions as easily as she could berate. Selvan felt miserable about not being able to bring her the smallest joy of a special gift and his despair doubled when he asked her one night, 'Don't you feel angry with me anymore?'

'Angry? For what?' she asked with surprise.

'For many things.' Selvan did not know for how many reasons she could be cross with him.

'No, never,' she said and tapped his head lightly as though he were being silly.

'Not even for not getting you a gift, not taking you to Ooty or buying you jasmine. Would you like me to sing for you today?'

She laughed aloud. And then lowering her voice said solemnly, 'I would never say "No" to anything you would do for me. But you don't have to try so hard to make me happy. It doesn't matter for I am happy already. I don't want to spend the days that you are here by getting annoyed and raising issues. These days with you are the best days in my life and I love them even without the gifts, jasmine, and outings.'

There was genuinely no grievance in her heart.

Selvan looked at her admiringly and wondered when she had attained such maturity. When had she grown so wise and wonderful in her views? She was still childlike but was not vulnerable. She still liked to be treated with care but did not seem fragile as before. She had evolved from a nubile nineteen-year-old to a compliant thirty-year-old. Time had taught her lessons in acceptance, and she seemed so much at peace with herself, despite the deprivations that she was enduring in her life. She never asked him if he could stay back forever or talked about the child that never would be born to them or expressed her little cinematic fantasies.

Finally, the day of his departure arrived. At the entrance to the departure lounge at the airport the atmosphere was one of gloom than glee. People bade farewell over tears, sobs and restraint, and then went about their ways.

Selvan hugged his mother, brothers and sisters, and gave the sisters-in-law a gentle nod of farewell and turned to Mangalam. She looked at him with aching eyes, unsure of what to say to him, only hoping that she held her restraint until he disappeared from view inside the airport.

'Come with me,' said Selvan taking her urgently by the elbow. He dragged her to a corner of the porch, away from the sniffling crowd, unmindful of his family's quizzical gaze and startled expression on Mangalam's face and said haltingly, 'I am so proud that you are being so calm. I don't want the tears to flow down, not even after I have gone. Remember, no matter how much my family tears my affections asunder, your share will always remain unscathed. It is special and yours forever.'

And then prizing out a shopping bag from his hand baggage and thrusting it into her hand he said, 'This is for you. I had wanted to give it to you all these days, but I did not because as you say, it doesn't matter anymore. But I can't take it back as there is no one else I can give it to. I bought it especially for you. I hope you do not hate me when you find what is inside. If you find it...' he paused searching for words, '...indecent and worthless, throw it away. I will find a better way of letting you know how much I think of you when I am away.'

'No, I liked it very much,' whispered Mangalam, holding back her tears. 'By the time you come next, I promise to grow thin enough to wear it,' she added with a wistful smile that gave her welling tears a gentle nudge. He looked at her in disbelief.

'Did you know?'

She nodded timidly.

The announcement for passengers to proceed for security intruded into their intense moments. Selvan took Mangalam's hand and gave it a squeeze. And then turning away, he waved to his family perfunctorily and wheeled the trolley in. Inside he turned again briefly to catch the hazy impression of Mangalam clutching the special gift to her heart.

CHAPTER THREE

Evil Predator

The first thing that Madhu heard from her cousin, Himani, upon landing in Dubai was this:

You are in an alien land. And completely free. Beware of what you do with your life here. You get only one chance. You mess it up and you are gone.

It wasn't possible for Madhu to gather the full import of what Himani had said, especially after a midnight flight and a long trudge through the mazy sprawl of the Dubai Airport, but she nodded perfunctorily. The only thing that she understood as she loaded her flaccid airbag into the boot of the taxi was that she was now on the threshold of a new life. A life different from the one she had led in Colombo. It was as if she was facing a new dawn, full of possibilities and promises, after a long stormy night that had seemed to never stall only a few months ago.

Even through the grogginess propelled by sudden change, she felt overwhelmed by the enormity of the change in her life. Away from home, separated from her daughter– she had landed in Dubai, in search of a future. A future that seemed non-existent until recently. She felt grateful to her cousin for bringing in this new season in her life.

As the taxi sped through the broad highways, Madhu took in the city and its grandeur, its many colours and charm. She was amazed at the surrealistic quality of the waning night, the intermingling of tranquility and vibrancy in the surroundings and slightly awed at the only thing that she could remember of her cousin's opening counsel – you are in an alien land. She closed her eyes to shut out the striking sights as the strangeness of the city suddenly gripped her. As she breathed deeply to let out the disquiet in her stomach, she inhaled the smell of perfume and sweat left behind by earlier passengers in the taxi. She felt nauseated. The speed and the smoothness of the drive aggravated the sudden feeling of sickness and she put her hand to her mouth instinctively, as if on the verge of retching.

'Can't you drive a little slow? And turn the AC on, please.' Himani said a tad curtly and loudly to the taxi driver as she opened a water bottle for Madhu.

The driver threw an irritated look at Himani through the rear-view mirror.

'It is on already. What more can I do? You know that it is peak summer. You madams just command as though you are some mudir and I am your personal driver. Why don't you buy your own car if you consider yourself so important?'

The odd accent and the gruff voice made him sound more arrogant than what he might have meant to.

Himani could read the driver's thoughts as he continued to vent his ire at his passengers, at the city, at his work and at his life. It seemed as though he was now merely voicing the bitterness that he had silently been carrying in his innards. His voice soon became a mumble and it got lost in the Hindi remix song playing on the tape.

'These taxi drivers are hassled people; their complaints are unending. He is merely peeved that even though our condition is no better than theirs, we behave like their masters when we are in the passenger's seat. As fellow aliens scrimping by in this desert land, they have plenty of grouse to voice,' Himani whispered suppressing a chortle. 'But let me tell you they are not so naïve. Give them half a chance and they will drive all over you. I will tell you more about them later,' Himani's tone was much lower and grave now, as she glanced deviously between the rear-view mirror and Madhu.

Madhu wondered why her cousin had to tell her more about taxi drivers and their manner.

'Actually, they are evil predators. You must be really careful,' Himani said as an afterthought, her voice now bordering on the ominous.

Madhu reached for the water bottle across Himani once again and felt tempted to take a peek at the mirror, more out of playful curiosity than any apprehension rising out of Himani's pronouncement about the evil predators.

It was only for an instant that she looked into the mirror, and she was met in the eye by the driver. Madhu, shocked at the unexpected encounter, tore her glance away in a hurry, her heart in the mouth.

'Which street?' the driver asked his eyes still in the mirror.

Madhu looked out the window, wondering if the man in front had caught her stealing a glance at him. Evil predators. Himani's words rang in her ears as she heard Himani give instructions. This time the words carried an odd resonance and she felt a strange sense of dread creep up her feet. A dread that was in some ways different from what she had felt in the past in Sri Lanka.

Outside a closed cafeteria, Madhu waited warily a few meters behind Himani as she paid the taxi driver. Through the corner of her eye Madhu strained to see traces of an evil predator in his face, but the darkness and his facial hair made it difficult to make an instant judgment. She sought comfort in the thought that darkness would have made it difficult for the man to see her face clearly too in the mirror.

Within two minutes the taxi veered away and zoomed out of view.

Madhu and Himani walked for five minutes along the pavement, passing by a twenty-four-hour petrol station and residential buildings that had shops and cafeterias on the ground floor.

'Where is your flat?' asked Madhu, surprised that they hadn't got off the taxi in front of Himani's home.

'In the street on the right, just two minutes away,' she said curving her palm outwards to indicate the turn to the right.

'Then why..?

Before Madhu could complete, Himani smiled wickedly and said, 'So that he wouldn't know where we stay.'

Himani said that it was a common trick all expatriate women, especially those living alone, played on taxi drivers.

'By living alone I mean living without male company,' she clarified. 'Remember, we have nobody to defend or protect us here. Therefore, we are taken to be easy prey for their exploits. Not just us, any woman of our kind, especially those doing low paid jobs. Indian, Filipina... I am not telling these things so that you get frightened or paranoid. But I want you to be on guard, at all times.'

Madhu smiled at her cousin, gratefully. She wanted to ask Himani especially about taxi drivers, were they so evil indeed? If so, how could they reach home safe at such unearthly hours? If only he had wanted, he could have taken them anywhere, done anything he so wished. Anything.

'You mean they even...' she said turning to look at Himani and suddenly stopped, her mind not wanting to stretch to the words of rape and murder.

'No, no... that sort of thing doesn't happen generally,'Himani said categorically knowing at once what her cousin had in mind. 'The law here takes care of that. One can't get away after doing such heinous things here. That is the greatest blessing in this place. But most of these men, and I just don't mean these taxi guys, but any other from other countries, are starved. You know what I mean by starved? These men don't have a family here, like us. No female company. So they find their own discreet means of satisfying their manly needs.'

Madhu felt the contempt and distaste in Himani's voice rasp her skin, wrapping her in a cloak of goose pimples.

By now they had entered a building, barely maintained or cleaned, the walls pealing, the stairs littered with crushed paper tissues, soda cans and toffee wrappers. Trails of brown spots - that looked more like bloodstains – left by dripping garbage bags completed the collage on the floor. Madhu was surprised that Dubai could have such sullied buildings too and she made her thoughts known to Himani.

'Never thought it could be like this in Dubai. Why doesn't anyone clean the building?'

'Who cares? Who cares about how we live? By the way, this is Sharjah, not Dubai. They are two different emirates,'

Himani said as she turned the key in and pushed the door open.

Madhu nodded as though she understood the difference.

They entered a hall to the right of which was a room with its door closed. A pair of hearts shaded with pink was pasted to the door. Before Madhu could ask her cousin anything, Himani said, 'I share this flat with two girls from Kerala. This hall is ours while that room is theirs. And the kitchen and bathroom are common. You can have just normal acquaintance with them, no need for over friendliness. These Malayali girls are very clever, and they have a sense of superiority.'

'What do they do?'

'One works in a beauty parlour and the other one is an assistant with a dentist.'

And then lowering her tone Himani said, 'Not the right kind. They sometimes bring men home. But I don't give a damn, whatever they do in their territory is their business.'

'Don't you have any, male friends?' asked Madhu hesitantly. She thought about the gossips that did the rounds in their village about Himani when she failed to return from Dubai even four years after she had left Sri Lanka. Himani had written to her family that she did not have enough money to pay for the tickets and that had evoked even more ridicule. Someone in Dubai being short of money was inconceivable to them. If people in Dubai didn't have enough money, who did? And so, it was concluded that she had 'something' that kept her tethered there. A man or even a love child.

'Boyfriends? Easiest to get but that's one thing I have kept myself safely away from. Illicit relationships are punishable by law here and I want no such danger in my life. No mood for such adventure as love, you could say.

Now can we catch some sleep? My day begins at six,' Himani said as she spread a comforter wide enough for two to sleep on.

Madhu watched her cousin switch the air conditioner on, gather her hair up into a mop and sink to the floor. 'Switch the lights off before you go to sleep,' she said as she curled up.

The cool gust of air from the noisy, old air conditioner filled the room and Madhu looked out into the street and beyond through the window.

Out there was a world where predators prowled, where it was easy to find boyfriends, where illicit love could get one behind bars. It was also a world that held promises, proffered hope, and sustained the lives of innumerable starry-eyed men and women.

Madhu felt a gentle chill catch at the tip of her fingers. She had so many things to get used to – the gust from the air conditioner, it's odd whirring noise, the heat outside, the girls in the other room, the single men with manly needs and many other things that she hadn't yet heard or known of this strange, new place.

Madhu was not used to being a housemaid. It was a job that she had never imagined taking up, not even in the worst of times back home. It wasn't the cleaning, scrubbing, and baby-sitting that disconcerted her, but the subservience she faced in the hands of those to who she was merely a housemaid. Not a human, not a woman, but a just a servant who did their bidding. But now, it was her only choice. Her cousin had advised her from the outset, from the time she had asked her to get her a visa to Dubai that a housemaid's job was all that she could expect to find there. She had agreed, for it was her only priority to find work of any kind and the prospect of finding work in Dubai obliterated the disgrace of being a housemaid until reality hit her hard.

Initially, it hurt her pride immensely to be at the beck and call of people whose language she barely understood, of temperamental women who screamed as if they were seized with madness, of conceited men who gave her only a slave's worth and of children who were just about as old as her own daughter yet called her by name or even worse, used mere interjections to call her.

Vexed and driven to utter frustration, she considered going back to her native village every second day, but a rigorous round of counselling from Himani and the question, what would she do if she returned, kept her back every time.

In the night, she would think of her home or whatever was left of it. Indeed, what would she do if she went back? How would she feed her daughter and mother? As Himani had once told her, this was her only chance at life and having no alternative, she clung to it hard, taking in the frequent abuses, regular reproach, and rare gestures of compassion as equably as she could. On days when her emotions breached the banks of her heart, she wept alone standing next to the window in her room, watching the world pass by. A world in which she did not belong yet could not tear away from owing to obligations back home.

How suddenly and drastically things in her life had changed! All it took was a loud noise, a ball of fire and a cloud of smoke to bring her world crashing in the middle of a market where she had gone with her husband, Ranjan, one summer afternoon. The sight of lifeless torsos, severed limbs, and bloodied bodies continued to haunt her sleep even today. The boom rang in her ears over the din and dust of the city and it made her rue the moment when she left him for a few minutes to go and fetch the bag she had left in the shoe shop some distance away. Nothing could wipe out the memories of the nemesis that left her howling in the midst of a flesh and blood ridden street, searching for Ranjan.

Even now, the sound of sirens and of human shrieks returned when a beacon flashing police vehicle or an ambulance passed by and it made her freeze as though her body had become one solid mass of ice. Seized with dread she would sink to the ground, gasping and fighting the macabre memory and wait for the panic to pass. Soaked in sweat and still panting, she would goad herself back to normalcy, cursing at the same time the sinister fate that left her to live. And then she would cry, knowing that was all she could do presently. She couldn't even contemplate suicide, with her mother and daughter back home pinning their life on her. She was all they were left with.

It took almost a year and half for Madhu to find some semblance of peace and happiness at work. After changing employers many times in that period, after being a part of many households, after many part-time and full-time stints, she found the Sharma family. An Indian doctor couple with a teenage daughter who had been in Dubai for over twenty years, their home became her haven during the day. She wasn't loathe to serve them, for she felt belonged when they endearingly called her Madhubeta, when their daughter shared stories from school and asked her about Sri Lanka, her home and family about which Madhu concocted stories, when Madam as she called Mrs. Sharma, taught her to cook Indian food, when she learnt words in Hindi which she carefully strung to make meaningful sentences within six months, when she accepted Madam's old dresses without feeling offended and eventually when the entire house was left in her care during the day when they were all out at work and school.

Even Himani covertly expressed her jealousy at the freedom Madhu enjoyed in the Sharma household, for trust, they knew, was a rare commodity in an alien place.

'Good for you. But be cautious, it is a huge responsibility. It takes no time for the belief they have in you to break. One suspicious act from you and its all gone. Don't even think of using their cot to sleep in, for they have means to know it. The most you can do is to watch TV. That's the maximum freedom you have at your disposal in their absence apart from work,' said Himani throwing a furtive glance of envy at her cousin. 'And don't even think of pinching anything from there. Any disrepute that you bring on is going to affect me directly. Let me be clear about that. It is on my assurance that they took you in.'

'No, I won't,' said Madhu calmly, at once pleased and aware of Himani's simmering envy. She was also conscious of the fact that all that Himani said wasn't entirely untrue. Freedom and trust came with great responsibility, and she had to commit herself to it for the sake of both herself and her cousin who had got her this far in Dubai. She owed that much to Himani.

It hadn't rained so heavily ever since Madhu came to Dubai. Himani said that it was the wettest day she had seen in the desert country. Almost like monsoon in Sri Lanka, she said, pouring in continuous drizzles and sometimes lashing down heavily.

'But where are the trees, hills, and rivers?'Madhu asked not relishing the reference to the monsoon in Sri Lanka. 'It is different. This is just rain and that is monsoon.'

She relived in her mind the time when she once walked under an umbrella through the field with Ranjan before they were married, the wind carrying the umbrella away when in a moment of closeness they lost the grip, the sudden embrace that followed, then the long kiss and the blush that refused to leave her face for long after.

She thought of the paper boats her daughter loved to push into the tiny watercourses outside their home, her thrill when the rain sprayed in through the open window and wetted her face, the fragrance of earth, the magic, and romance of a season.

The rustic rain in her village, the urban deluge in Colombo and this strange torrent in the desert – she compared them as she stood by the window watching the road below getting waterlogged and cars splashing through them, honking and blinking with despair.

'Even the rain in this place looks artificial,' she said suddenly, turning towards Himani. 'As if forced to come down because it had obligations to keep. Like us.'

'I certainly have an obligation to go to work today. How about you? Spending the day watching the rain?' asked Himani as she prepared to go.

'I don't know. There seems to be a lot of water on the road.'

'Yes, there is. I think I will take a taxi today. But finding one in these conditions is going to be tough. They are all going to be engaged.'

Himani usually walked it down to her workplace and her persistent dislike – which sometimes bordered on paranoia – about travelling by taxis made her look for homes close by to work in. It wasn't easy for Madhu either to shrug off the vitriolic inputs her cousin had given her about taxi drivers, especially those who ran the private service, but she had gathered courage over a period of time to take a taxi, especially during summer when it was an ordeal to walk down even a kilometre. Although the rides weren't devoid of unsavoury episodes, she took them for want of an alternative.

True to Himani's words, the men at the wheel often tried to strike up conversations, some even trying to wheedle out personal details on her life. Having been sufficiently briefed by Himani, Madhu would be on guard, maintaining a grim face while in the taxi, often to a level that stressed her, giving no leeway to the man in front to go beyond the initial query on nationality.

She learnt that giving the men a cold shoulder was the best way to stave off any unseemly experience. So she would get on, turn her head towards the window and keep her eyes fixed outside as though taking in the city in all earnestness, never once trying to cast a glance at the driver. It had worked quite well with her.

Except once.

It was close to dusk and windy that day. The winter had closed in on the desert land in a manner that made the insufferable summer seem like a distant memory.

Waiting outside her employer's house, Madhu felt the chill creep up her feet, blow in through her ears and bite the tip of her nose. She had been out there waiting for a taxi for ten minutes, bearing the wind that kicked up columns of sand into the air. There was barely anyone walking on the road and Madhu felt awkward standing alone in the twilight, trying to wave down a ride home. She began to walk slowly after a couple of unsolicited drivers of private cars slowed down in front of her, honked for her attention and then drove away when she turned her face against them. She loathed the men who were so desperate to waylay a lonely woman on the road. She spared a few invectives for them in her thoughts and made her way along the pavement when a taxi pulled up close to her. Startled and jerked out of her thoughts, she stopped.

'Taxi?'

'Er...yes.'

Eager to seek shelter from the wind she bundled herself in hurriedly. Gritting her teeth she told him her destination, a street away from where she actually lived. She had never deviated from this practice that Himani had first taught her.

'Very cold, eh, Madam?' she heard the man say as soon as the car took off. She could make out from the driver's voice that he was beaming wide in his seat. Was it an expression of satisfaction over getting a woman passenger on a wintry evening or just a sadistic delight at seeing her tremble, wondered Madhu.

'When it is hot, it is as hot as an oven and when cold, it rips your skin apart,' he said veering into the fast track and tailgating a car in front. 'Why didn't you wear a sweater?

Two minutes into the drive and Madhu felt uneasy. The man was starting up a conversation, she concluded with loathing. But there was something that perturbed her more than the fact that the man had got jabbering. It was the drawl in his voice. There was something familiar in the way the words came out – rough and rugged. The accent was typical of men from Afghanistan. And she had heard it before.

'Where are you from? India?'

Madhu stayed silent. If that was what he thought, so be it.

'Indian women are very beautiful. I like them. I know an Indian lady, a nurse who goes to work by my taxi frequently. And there are many that I know. All beautiful. Nice ladies.'

Madhu cursed the moment when she had got on to the taxi. She considered getting off and taking another one, but the weather outside deterred her from doing so. She had to put up with the man and his rattle till she reached her destination. Much to her chagrin, the traffic moved very slow, making her impatient and frustrated.

'Where do you work?' the driver asked turning his head to the left and trying to catch her in view.

'Why do you want to know? You just drive and take me to my destination,' Madhu snapped back.

'Why are you getting annoyed, Madam? I was just chatting to pass time. If you don't want to tell me, that's fine. I thought you would be friendly like the other Indian women I know.'

'I am not Indian,' said Madhu suddenly and then regretted having revealed a lot more than what she needed to.

'No? You look like one. Now, I won't ask where you are from. You will again be angry... and what if you open the door and jump out!' he said good-naturedly and looked into the rear-view mirror followed by a quick laugh.

What exactly made Madhu look at the mirror in the same moment she didn't know, but when their eyes met... she knew. The pair of eyes in the mirror were the same she had stared into on their way from the airport nearly two years ago.

More than being amused at the coincidence, Madhu was surprised that she had remembered the man's eyes well enough to recognise. This time she saw them in the waning day light and caught the green in them. They were the most remarkable pair of eyes she had ever seen, especially in a man. She felt her breath quicken and her heartbeat to a displaced rhythm. She looked away for a few moments, in an effort to regain her calm and then returned to the mirror, but his eyes had moved away from its frame. They were on the road, moving along with the easing traffic, navigating his car through the maze of other vehicles. She was annoyed with herself for the disappointment she felt at not finding him in the mirror.

There was silence for some time and Madhu wished there was music playing to keep her disquiet down.

'Why do some women behave so rudely with us?' the driver said after a while, his coarse voice almost somber. It sounded as though he was merely thinking aloud, venting his thoughts.

'We taxi drivers are very talkative, I admit. What else is there to life, you tell me. Now you get angry because I talk too much, because I ask about you. But that's the only way we keep ourselves amused in this big city of the rich and powerful. It makes us happy to make a few friends here and there, friends who are like us—lonely, hardworking, but hearty. If being talkative is a crime, then I am a criminal and so are many others in this city, for words are the only things that connect us to this strange world of the super-rich and the utter poor from other places.'

Madhu wanted to say that was not true. He wasn't as naive as he made himself out to be. She knew that they were predators disguised as sweet talkers. They were starved for female company and preyed on lonely, unaccompanied women who were there because of obligations. And many women even complied willingly, as Himani had told her smugly, only because it gave their lives some added pleasure and colour.

'You know what? Sometimes I feel that people like us, and I don't mean you, are not human, we are mere animals brought to serve these rich men. We are mere donkeys. And where do the donkeys belong? In the stinking stables of these filthy rich men. Stables that reek of our sweat and toil, stables made foul by abuse and infested with our woes. Is it then so wrong to make a few alliances that bring in a whiff of freshness into our dingy, dirty existence?

'Do you see these tall buildings, Madam?' he continued unmindful of whether Madhu was clued in or not. 'They are supposed to make this country the best that can be in the entire world. But what does that mean to me...to you? What difference does it make to our life if more rich people fill this piece of earth? We have nothing here, except this sweat that breaks out of our skin even when the air conditioner is on. Nothing in this place bonds us except words and this sweat.'

Madhu listened to him this time, his spiel almost touching her heart. Nothing that he said was untrue. She looked out into the street that had by now fired up under the sodium vapour lamps. The glitter and the glamour, the prosperity and the power, the speed and the spirit meant nothing to her. At best, she partook of them by wearing a cheap perfume bought from the bargain shop, a pair of high-heeled shoes, and a skirt and blouse that did nothing beyond classifying her as typically Sri Lankan.

She remembered how once Mrs Sharma's daughter had said, 'You Sri Lankans have a typical way of dressing, don't you? One can know you from a distance. There is something strange about it.'

Madhu was not sure if it was a compliment, nevertheless she didn't like the way she was being stereotyped, although such labelling was neither new nor strange to her. How many times had she heard Himani talk of Malayali girls as being crafty, women from the far eastern countries being morally loose, taxi drivers and other bachelors from the subcontinent and above who traipsed the city on weekends being drooling donkeys!

She now noticed that the driver had stopped talking, probably from the sheer exhaustion of conducting a one-sided conversation. They were close to her home and as always, she asked him to stop a few blocks away. Try as she might, she couldn't shrug off the bizarre thought that some taxi guy would actually detect where she lived and follow her into the building. It was only one of the many threads of fear that she had imbibed from her cousin.

'Madam, you could call me should you need a taxi anytime. If I am anywhere in the vicinity, I will come along. Take my number,' the driver said as she handed him the fare. She avoided looking at his face although a part of her coaxed her to catch the green of his eyes one last time.

'Don't you want the number?' he asked again.

Madhu hesitated for a while, before taking her phone and punching in the number he read aloud. For some strange reason she could not spurn his suggestion to store his number although she knew she would never need it. She would never have to call a man who in her current estimation was between an evil predator and a hassled soul suffering from verbal dysentery.

On one hand, she was suspicious of his intentions. The fact that he had taken the liberty of giving her his contacts unnerved her; there was no apparent need for him to do that. She felt that he could even have meant something more devious than what he had said in words and calling him when in need for a ride could mean courting the very danger that Himani had always cautioned her about.

On the other hand, she felt a gentle throb of compassion in her sinews thinking of the man who spoke excessively only because he was bored with the limited life he led behind the wheels. As she had once heard someone say, other people's lives always made for interesting stories. He could merely be a man looking for some interesting stories to lend his tedious travails a touch of delight.

Unable to decide if the man who ferried her across the city was a trickster or an ordinary immigrant driver given to innocuous fun with his passengers, Madhu walked down, following the taxi with her eyes till it merged with the traffic and vanished from sight.

It was close to ten in the morning and Madhu finally made up her mind. The rains continued unabated, and it had taken more than half an hour for Himani to find a taxi. By the time she got into one, her clothes were drenched from feet upwards from both the rain and the splash from the passing traffic.

Madhu could have asked Mrs Sharma for a day's leave but even before she could do that, Mrs Sharma had called Madhu to say that she had to go that day, in spite of the bad weather. They were having guests for dinner and there was a heap of things to be done. Madhu felt a strange disgust for the guests and for Mrs Sharma. How could they party when there was so much rain outside, when it was such an ordeal to get there and when she so wanted to stay home, curl up and sleep?

We are mere animals serving the rich, she remembered the taxi driver saying and it filled her with instant spite for Mrs Sharma.

'I will surely be there by ten, Madam, don't worry,' she had said concealing her dismay. At that time she had no clue as to how she would wade through the water and rain to reach Madam's home.

She felt frustrated and looked out into the street again. Why didn't people ever think of others? Why didn't they consider the difficulties? How could they be so selfish? Party on a day like this! Didn't they have better things to do? She cursed and swore under her breath. And then after a few seething moments she decided.

She took the phone to make the call she never thought she would ever make. After typing in four digits, she paused, wondering what she would say. How would she describe herself to him? How would he know her from the scores of passengers he picked and dropped every day? Especially, if he had given them all his number which was very likely.

She spent five minutes pondering and then called.

'Taxi?'

'Yes, Madam.'

She described the location of her building and the place she wanted to go.

'Madam, it will take at least half an hour. I have a passenger right now.'

Madhu felt the rough intonated voice rasp on her ears and a pair of green eyes flashed in her mind.

'Okay, give me a call when you reach my place.'

She disconnected and stared at the phone, wondering at once if she had done the right thing by calling a taxi driver. He now had her number. If he was indeed the kind of man that Himani had warned her about, then she was in serious trouble. She felt her palm getting clammy and her breath quicken. She suddenly realised the magnitude of the mistake she had made. She was now exposed to a stranger who in the eyes of single women in this place was an evil predator.

She still had an option—she could choose not to go by his taxi. But that did not diminish the chances of her being in his list of prey. He had already got her number. Fretful and undecided, she peeped out of the window now and then and felt a leap in her heart every time a taxi passed by.

And then the phone rang. It was him, the caller ID flashed Taxi Driver, as she had recorded in her phone. She waited tentatively, swallowing emptily and staring at the phone. The ring stopped after a minute. She peered out of the window and saw a taxi pulling over to the opposite side of the street. And then the phone rang again. She lurched forward and switched the phone on instinctively.

'Hello,' she whispered still shaking with panic. She failed to fathom what had made her take the call.

'Madam, where are you? Which building? I am already at the spot you gave me.'

'Yes, I am coming in two minutes.'

Madhu wondered what goaded her on even when her brain frantically sent out ominous signals. She had no time to think. The only way to reach Madam's house was this and she had to take it, if she had to keep her job. For all the niceties that Madam showed towards her, she was unbending and brooked no slackness at work.

Madhu had to go. She picked her bag and left. Nothing untoward would happen, she promised herself. It was just an odd occasion, and it merited no serious apprehension. It was after all only a taxi ride like the many rides she had taken before.

Madhu saw the familiar face partially covered with beard as she crossed the road.

'Madam, you? What a surprise!' the driver said with a beaming smile as she got in.

Madhu managed to give a wan, feigned smile in response.

'Is this where you live?'

'Yes.'

'But the other day I dropped you before the turning there.'

'I lived there then,' Madhu lied quickly.

'Going to work?'

'Yes.'

'Where?'

'In a house.'

The driver didn't seem surprised by her reply. He merely nodded in acknowledgment.

'I know another Indian lady who works in the house of an Arab.'

'I am not Indian.' Madhu corrected him.

'No? Really? I thought you were joking the other day

'No, I am Sri Lankan.'

'But you all look similar, Indians, Sri Lankans,' he said looking into the rear view mirror.

The green eyes again. Madhu looked away in a hurry. She wondered how much of her he could view in the reflection on the mirror.

'Been here for long?'

'A few years,' said Madhu off-handedly, not wanting to give him precise replies while not wanting to sound rude either.

'I am from Afghanistan and I have been here for twelve years. Do you know Afghanistan?'

Madhu nodded realising that he was viewing her in the mirror. She had heard of Afghanistan but didn't know much about the place.

'From Afghanistan I came over to Pakistan first. Peshawar. That is where I learned driving first. Spent a few years there before coming here... You have a family?'

'Yes.' She didn't bother to say more.

'I have too, a big one – parents, brothers, sisters, uncles, aunts – but I haven't met them for twelve years. Many of those who I left behind are not even alive now. Some of those alive are in Afghanistan surviving the war, some are in Pakistan, in refugee camps. Our family is completely broken. This continuing war has wrecked us all.'

Madhu caught the gloom in his voice. She thought of her home and almost said, I haven't been home either since I came here. War wrecked my home too... but she was stopped by a sudden brake that made her lurch forward.

'Sorry. It is a rough drive today because of the rain. How will you return? I can come and pick you if you let me know. I don't insist, I just thought of offering, that's all. '

Madhu smiled as if to say, that's alright, I will manage my way back.

When she got off in front of the Sharma residence, she knew that the man in the taxi wasn't so evil after all.

'Thanks,' she said with a smile that absolved the man of his excesses. And then for once, she looked at him and the green eyes from the front. She wondered what he might look like without the dense beard that swathed a big part of his face. It only made him look savage, dangerous and intimidating, which he probably was not.

'Let me know if you need my services. By the way, my name is Armaan. It means desire in our language,' he said with a smile.

Madhu wondered if she should reciprocate by giving him her name. Not this time, she decided.

Later that evening, she added the name of Armaan in her phonebook against his number. He wasn't merely the taxi driver now.

Initially, they met at least twice a week.

Armaan would pick Madhu up from near Madam's house and they would spend time in a restaurant or a park. It wasn't possible for them to meet in the open where the passers-by gave them an amused look. It wasn't common to see a pathan and a woman from somewhere around the sub-continent sitting together.

And then there were the prying cops who were on the lookout for people indulging in immoral activities. What was immoral about two people being in love, Madhu failed to understand, but the law of the land prohibited any such liaison, and they were wary of being picked up for questioning. That gave them very less time to spend in each other's company, with Madhu insisting that he dropped her home before the sun set.

They often disagreed over this issue, but somehow Madhu had her way in the end. Armaan left her in front of her building and waited till she went up and waved from the window. And he would feel surprised all over again at having found her. It wasn't that there haven't been women in his life, but none of them were for love.

There was very less physical contact between them, the deterrent being the law rather than their self-restraint. He held her hand every time they were in the car and even managed to shift gears with her hand in his, and that she said, was the only luxury she could allow him.

Once when he tried to reach out from his seat to kiss her, she pushed him so hard on the face that her nails scratched his skin bloody. But for the windows that were rolled up, her shriek could have caught the attention of bystanders and pedestrians.

'It could have got both of us in serious trouble, do you know,' he said gravely, in mock annoyance.

She took his hand in hers, locked their fingers and then apologised. She hadn't meant to raise an alarm. She just wasn't prepared for anything more than simple things.

It was unfair, he said, to be in love and be constrained. On many such occasions when she sat beside him, he felt an irresistible urge to lean over and grab her, but he held back knowing too well that it would only jeopardise their relationship. He knew that she would come around someday, and so he waited.

Whenever they met, twice a week, they spent time talking about their past, their present and when things came to their future, they stopped. What was their future? Where would they go from here in their love? These were questions that neither of them had answers for.

'Shall we get married?' he asked her once.

They sat overlooking the beach, the windows of the car rolled down just enough to let the breeze in.

She looked at him, her eyes full of surprise and excitement for one moment and then a pall of sudden gloom falling across her face and stealing the glint of her eyes.

'You are joking, really?'

'No, I want to marry you. Will you convert to my religion?'

Marriage, conversion – these were things she hadn't contemplated about, not even when she realised that she was completely in love with Armaan. It seemed too overwhelming for her to even consider these things in her life. She couldn't think of a new life with Armaan, not with Anu and her mother back home. Not with the memories of Ranjan's tragic death still haunting her. But then what had she expected of her relationship with Armaan? Was it just a romantic interlude in her life? As she groped through the cobwebs of her brain searching for answers, she felt Armaan's breath close to her face. She stared into the green eyes, waiting apprehensively.

'Armaan, how can we marry? Here, where we don't belong, where the law is against us, where we have no status. How can I marry? What will happen to Anu and Amma back home?' she whispered.

'Do you want to marry me?'

'Yes.'

'Then we shall, Insha Allah. Some day we shall marry,' said Armaan leaning forward.

'Armaan, we must go,' she said leaning backwards, trying to evade him.

Anything could happen in that twilight hour, she knew. She did not trust herself. She felt an urge to push Armaan back, open the door of the car and run towards the sea. She saw the setting sun behind Armaan and the horizon that beckoned her. It seemed far away. She wished she could reach there, merge with it so that it would absorb all the uncertainty in her mind – about Armaan, his love, their future and the hopelessness she suffered every time she thought of a life together. But she felt immobile, her limbs refused to stir, and she sat, waiting for the inevitable to happen, against her own code and her will, and then giving in to her instincts, slipped into a dream.

She heard him speak softly into her ears – endearments in his native Pashto that Madhu barely understood – the warmth of his breath wafting over her face, his facial hair tickling her skin and she knew that the predator had eventually got her. Despite her caution, despite her denials.

It was now getting increasingly difficult for Madhu to meet Armaan, especially after he took up the new job.

When the government decided to take private taxis off the road after a slew of complaints from passengers about poor maintenance, service, and uncouth behaviour, Armaan applied for a job with the government transport company and being a seasoned driver with ten years' experience, he was selected. That meant longer, more stringent working hours with no time to spare for Madhu.

Those were the days of torment for Madhu. Parallel to the shamaal that raged outside, ripping the desert and tossing dust into the air, a storm brewed in Madhu's heart, torn between the guilt, joy, and fear of what she had done with Armaan behind the dark curtains of dusk.

The thought of how perilous an act it had been made her shudder every time she revisited the experience in her mind. Almost in the open, with a man who immigrant women would at best describe as sleazy, voluble and on the prowl, in a country that forbid the slightest display of affection in public, without the tiniest fear of being discovered – it had been boldness carried to the extremes. But that is what love does – she rationalised in her moments of guilt. It fogs the mind, makes the heart unbelievably intrepid, wipes shame off the mind, and gives the delight of a lifetime.

She could not dismiss the indescribable pleasure that it was—more for the soul than the body, more by its earnestness than by its passion, more by the manner it began than by the way it culminated. It made her feel as if she were levitating. The memory of the frenzy, the cadence and the fulfillment filling every cell of her being, making her want more of him, making her want to gather the most of his love before the uncertainty of the future caught up with them.

In moments of loneliness and longing in her room she thought of Armaan's words, Insha Allah, someday we shall marry. And his word was her only hope, her Armaan.

However, with the reduced frequency of their meetings, she felt sinister thoughts crowding her mind in clusters. Was it a mistake? Had she been hasty? What would become of her should Armaan desert her? Was he really an evil predator who would discard her heart after savouring her flesh?

She tried to convince herself that her mind was playing tricks on her and that Armaan wasn't an evil predator. He couldn't be, not after the mutual sharing of their sorrows in life, not after seeing the pain of the past in each other's eyes and certainly not after having given her a taste of his intimacy.

'I am afraid, Armaan. I am afraid you are casting me out of your life. I spend night after night thinking of it. Why don't you see me?' she said every time she spoke to him on phone. The calls he made were the only comfort she had, the only sign of his loyalty towards her. But she was not assuaged.

'How do I explain to you? I spend hours and hours caught in the Dubai traffic, trying to meet my target for the day. You know it. It is not like earlier times when time was at my disposal. I could forego a few passengers for your sake, but now there are the rules in the company. You understand, don't you? You understand that I love you, don't you?'

Madhu understood but her heart was relentless. It needed more proof, it needed certification, and it saw nothing beyond her love for him and her urgent need to be with him.

'I understand, but I want you to promise me that you are not forsaking me. If you do I will die and I promise I will,' said Madhu. Her tone was more somber than menacing.

'Don't be silly. Is that what you have thought of me? How could you?'

'Then tell me you will see me this week....no... tomorrow.'

'Tomorrow?'

'Yes, tomorrow. I have something important to tell you. You either see me or I go and slash my wrist.'

'Alright, alright. I will see you tomorrow. You tell me where and promise me that you will not even mention unspeakable things like taking your life. God never pardons those who even think of it.'

'I promise,' Madhu whispered into the phone. She knew she wasn't merely threatening Armaan with a suicide should he abandon her at any point of time, yet she made a promise to him. 'Come to Madam's house tomorrow. They will be away until evening. I can't of think any other place.'

'There? That's dangerous and not right either.'

'What's dangerous Armaan? What is not right? For two people in love to meet? Then where do all men and women in this place go to share their love? I have had enough of this. I need to talk, to spend time with you. Is that asking for too much?'

'All right, calm down. I will be there tomorrow between eleven and eleven thirty in the morning. If there is any change, I will call you.'

'There won't be a change, Armaan. I will wait for you,' she disconnected the phone curtly.

It was a moment of reckoning for her and in that moment, Armaan was her only truth in life. Everything else – her past, its memories, her obligations, her roots – seemed like dull, peripheral aspects. She was incapable of even recognising the absurdity of it.

In the hours that followed, Madhu was completely consumed by the excitement of a clandestine meeting in Madam's house. Only the thrill of being with Armaan filled her thoughts, only his amorous whispers rang in her ears.

Strangely, she felt no fear. She knew they were safer in the confines of Madam's house than anywhere else. And it wasn't every day that she took such liberty. She had been a trustworthy and hard-working housemaid, and she could award herself some freedom, in their absence of course.

She chose the latest dress that she had in her wardrobe – a flowing, red skirt and white full sleeved blouse. On days that she met Armaan, she made it a point to wear clothes that covered her completely, just to please him. Covering her head had often been a matter of argument between them for it meant a change more than she could presently accept.

'Wear a hijab. I don't like you going around like this,' he would say often.

But Madhu said it would make people suspicious, especially her cousin and employers. What she didn't openly mention was her unpreparedness for it. She still couldn't completely come to terms with the thought of having to change her faith. She still needed to be convinced that she could embrace a new religion for the sake of love. She didn't dismiss it entirely but felt hesitant, and convinced Armaan that she would do it gradually. She merely needed time.

She dressed with extra interest for her meeting with Armaan, sprucing up yet not overdoing. She waited for her cousin to leave for work and then examined her face in the wall mirror. Somehow, her unthreaded eyebrows, the dark rings under her eyes and a few blemishes left behind by pimples seemed more pronounced than other times. Dismayed, yet emboldened by the thought that it wasn't her first date after all, she dabbed her face with powder, lined her eyes, and coloured her lips lightly. As she brushed her long hair that fell to her waist, she remembered Armaan telling her, 'You have such beautiful hair. It makes me a hopeless romantic.'

He wasn't the first person to say that. Ranjan had often said in jest that he had fallen in love with her hair first and then with her. Madhu wondered what it was about long tresses that made men go weak in their knees.

Though the day was cloudy and cool, walking to Madam's house would make her exhausted. It would also ruin her gentle make-up. So she took a taxi. As it inched through the congested roads that left no scope for overtaking, she became aware of her nervousness, impatience, and anxiety. Nervous like a teenager going on a secret date, impatient like a woman waiting for her beloved, and anxious like a bride before her nuptials.

It took fifteen minutes for her to reach Madam's house. She wished no one from Madam's house saw her getting off a taxi or noticed her dapper appearance. To her luck, only Madam was home when she walked in. Her daughter and husband had already left.

Running late, Madam too left in a hurry ten minutes after Madhu's arrival. She barely acknowledged Madhu, only rattling off instructions from her bedroom to her distracted and tense maid in the kitchen. Madhu fumbled with the dishes and dropped one on her toes. It was only on her departure that Madhu felt her breathing return to normal, only to gather pace again as time passed.

She did not know what to expect, her thoughts doing cartwheels, now excited, now calm. Fearful one moment, complacent the other. She felt odd that after so many months, several meetings, and a relationship almost stabilised by consent and understanding, she was feeling nervous about seeing him. She felt a sense of foreboding somewhere in the cranny of her mind. She pushed the thoughts out and shut the doors of her mind tight.

At eleven, she dropped her chores and stood near the window, waiting for the beige car to pull up. And it did at quarter past eleven. Madhu watched Armaan, looking dapper in his uniform and newly trimmed beard walking up. She acknowledged his transformation from a rather seedy taxi driver to a well-groomed cabby with a smile when her phone rang. She directed Armaan to the flat on the fourth floor and waited behind the door.

'Was there anyone in the elevator? Did anyone see you coming?' she asked as soon as he came in.

'There wasn't anyone in the elevator. But I don't know if anyone saw me. Does that bother you?'

'No, not really. I was just curious,' she said and turned to go in to fetch a cold drink.

'I have only half an hour, Madhu. I came only because you threatened me with...' she heard Armaan's words trail off behind her.

She sensed the impatience in his voice and wondered if he wasn't happy to be there. He didn't seem half as excited as her. On the other hand, his manner betrayed some degree of irritation that disquieted her.

'Okay. I just wanted to see you and tell you something. You can go in half an hour. But tell me, why weren't you seeing me all these days?'

'You can't ask me the same question every day. You know I don't find the time.'

'No time for me? Or no time to see me?' Madhu hoped that Armaan knew the difference between the two. She also hoped that he hadn't found her question more caustic than what she had intended it to be.

She had almost asked him if he had dumped her, left her to live with memories of a phony affair and was pleased that she hadn't. It could have strained those moments of togetherness. She swallowed her worry about Armaan's earnestness with a few quick slurps of mango juice.

'You know I love you, don't you?' Armaan said suddenly grabbing her by the wrist.

'Don't say that unless you really do,' Madhu said quickly and winced as Armaan's grip around her wrists tightened. His sudden fierce manner alarmed her, and she tried to twist her hands free.

'You wouldn't hurt me if you loved me,' she said grimacing.

'Here, I let you go. But I love you. You are unlike any other woman who has been in my life. Quite unlike. With them it was never love, but with you it is. You don't trust me? You don't, do you? I want to prove it. I want to prove it to you time after time. Will you let me? Will you let me prove it to you?'

Armaan's sudden frenzy startled Madhu. She became aware of what the moment demanded of her, and she stepped back, unable to decide. Before she could make sense of what was happening to her, Armaan appeared in front of her, clasping her by the shoulder and crushing her into his chest.

Caught in a whirlwind of passion, she surrendered, like she did the first time in the car on the beach. She felt herself break to smithereens, each fragment demanding more of Armaan. As they transcended the realms of love within the four walls of Madam's house, there was no fear of the law, the guilt of an illicit liaison or the coyness, of an incipient relationship. She felt as if she were gliding, in the vast blue sky, miles above the desert sand, viewing the tiny world of the rich below with contempt.

When the doorbell rang, she sprang up in horror, hastened with her clothes and exclaimed, 'Armaan, we are finished.'

'Who could it be?' he asked, numb with fear.

'I don't know. It could be the caretaker,' she said hoping it was indeed him. If so they were in no danger. He would go away after waiting for a couple of minutes assuming the house to be locked.

But the bell rang again. Madhu walked gingerly up to the door and peered through the eyehole. What she saw outside filled her with instant dread. It was Madam.

Madhu flitted back to Armaan and urged him to hide.

'But where?'

Just then her mobile phone began to ring, flashing Madam's name. She looked around, panic turning her face white and pushing her eyes out. And then in a flash she saw Armaan dash towards the balcony. She ran after him and before she realised it, he had put his leg over the railing. Madhu gasped and screamed loud, her hand on her mouth as she saw Armaan flip over and fall. A shriek and then a thud four floors below. Madhu staggered and slumped on the balcony floor. She struggled to breathe, and her eyes stung. She shut her eyes tight, and darkness embraced her...

She felt a cloud of smoke engulf her. There were burning vehicles, blown bodies and blood on the street. She heard the deafening noise of human cries and sirens. And then the darkness fell again but this time there was silence.

Somewhere behind the chaos of death and devastation, beyond the silence that beckoned, a doorbell rang frantically along with a tune from a mobile phone.

CHAPTER FOUR

The Disguise

Ramayya examined his dark, sun burnt skin once again before applying the silver paint on his body. The blotches on the skin left behind by constant exposure to the sun were growing and they were beginning to hurt. Soon they would invade his whole being, and slowly he would die.

It was a thought that had been recurring in his mind ever since he spotted the first patch on his arm. And then they appeared on his neck, his cheek, and his back (as discovered by his wife one evening when she was scrubbing the paint off). The blisters were breaking into the surface at an alarming speed, and he would not have many more days out there in the open. His retirement time would soon be upon him, he thought wanly. The children were yet to come off age and the thought of finding an alternative occupation to support his family vexed him.

He took the paint in his hand, gave it a hard stare, and then began to smear it on his body. It spread like butter on an over done toast, and soon, he was swathed in his new gleaming, silvery look. He looked in the mirror and touched up his face. The eyes were the most difficult part to do.

'See if it is done on the back,' he said to his wife, Rukku.

'We have had enough of this. Why don't you just stop this madness? I can't take it anymore,' she said, as she had always done in the past, and then resignedly touched the paint in places that he had left out. Little islets of brown skin got submerged in a deluge of silver. She sniffled as she painted her husband up from a live human being to a lifeless statue.

'What else do you expect me to do? Go around begging?' he asked.

There was no way to dissuade him.

'This is no better than begging,' she said wryly. 'Have you thought of us ever?' she asked. 'What would happen if you collapsed one day in the middle of the town?'

'Thought of you, you ask? Who else am I doing this for? And you call this begging? Begging means to put your hand out to others and I am doing no such thing,' he said firmly.

He was very proud of what he was doing for a living. His pride hurt and he seethed with anger whenever he was compared to an alms taker. He had his rationale to whatever he did: he did not extend his hand; he did not look pathetic and impoverished, nor did he bawl out in distress. He merely had found a new means of getting people's attention, an unusual way of gaining their compassion and a unique manner of making a living by tapping into their sensibility and nationalistic feeling.

In his own self-respecting view, he was going to work, a work like no one else.

'You need to be proud of what I am doing,' he said to Rukku.

She looked into his eyes, a glistening island of life in a sea of silver paint and nodded wistfully. Ramayya wished he could take her hand or better still, hold her close and assure her that he would not die on the streets, that the sun or the paint would not kill him.

He wished he could say it, even if as a travesty, but the paint on his body prevented any such kindly gesture and so leaving her to seek her own comfort, he ambled out.

From mid-morning till afternoon, a period when the sun pounds down its full blaze on earth, he would be on the streets of the temple town overwhelming tourists, enticing children and shoving down the throats of the local residents their daily dose of patriotic sentiment in a tacit but diligent manner.

He would be at the crossing close to the bus terminus for a while and then he would shift to the town square or the park during weekends, where he stood, (and he earned his living just standing still), for another two hours before walking back to his house. He would count his revenue for the day on his return, once in the evening and then again before going to bed and stash them away in the savings box inside the wooden cupboard. The earnings ebbed and flowed according to the season, sometimes choking his wooden box to its mouth and at other times leaving it dismally empty, but Ramayya quickly learned to grapple with the inconsistencies of his daily takings by maintaining an account and managing his money like a regular wage earner.

For some reason he never gave Rukku the real figures of his earnings and she did not suspect him of false disclosure either. She never felt the compulsion to do a clandestine check of his income or savings; it was sufficient that her husband was earning by honest means, although every once in a while, she was overcome by a feeling of lowliness and dejection about the method he adopted.

She still thought at times that it was only beggary in disguise.

Not many in the town knew his name. Fewer still knew where he lived or what he actually looked like. He had always been known by his disguise – the pose, the hairless pate, and the stick in his hand lending quality and genuineness to the silvery camouflage – and it has been his means to provide for his wife and three children for some time now. Since the time he took up the disguise as his livelihood, the family has not known scarcity, at least not the kind that they had suffered when he had lost his job as a sweeper in a factory and was left with no means to feed his family.

Those were grueling times when he was thrown out of his job after being wrongly accused of being involved in a theft in the factory. Oddly enough, everyone was convinced even without evidence that it was he who had filched away valuable material from the plant and shop floor. He wasn't even given a chance to prove his innocence. But then as he says, the poor don't ever get a chance.

'What do we do now?' asked Rukku tiredly, the day he returned home disgraced and emotionally battered by an overarching authority at his workplace that assumed his guilt without any trial or test.

'They called me a thief,' he said reprovingly rubbing his head in intense dismay. 'How could they? Will my house be like this if I had all the money they accuse me of making from selling the company's property? Will this be the way you will be clothed? Will this be the way we would live?'

'Didn't you tell them?' Rukku asked eagerly. Her face blazed with the hurt of the slander slapped on her husband.

'Why wouldn't I? But will they pay attention? They have decided to dump it on me, a poor sweeper. The real thief must be laughing in secret and counting his money,' Ramayya said with disgust. The invectives that followed were rarities in his everyday life that he reserved for especially coarse moments as these.

'I am sure he will get caught someday, and your innocence will be proved. Truth has never failed...'Rukku said with a resigned sigh. What more could a dutiful wife do in times as these except impart courage and hope to her man in distress? What else was within her means?

Ramayya shook his head. He had no hope, no faith in the justice of the rich and mighty. And now he had no job either. The few places he went to looking for a job, he was turned away owing to his newly earned disrepute.

'In this town, even news about sweepers gets across to the people as though we are the most important people around,' he said scornfully. 'There is no one ready to employ a thief... A thief, your husband. Did you know? Did you know that is what the entire town knows me now as? Isn't this unfair?'

Ramayya could not stop ranting as he stayed home nursing the disgrace for days together while his wife took up work as a domestic help in three houses.

So disillusioned was Ramayya that he eventually decided not to look for work anymore. Contrary to what his wife believed, it was a well thought of decision, one that steered him to consider new avenues and strange methods of earning a living.

'I am not going to be a sweeper anymore. Not going to work for anybody. I am going to be my own boss,' he declared one day.

His wife looked at him quizzically. She had grown immensely concerned about him in the days after he lost his job that saw him fritter away time at home tending to their children. She had allowed him a few days to recover from his depression, but when the convalescing period began to stretch indefinitely, she grew anxious.

She feared that he would take to vices – chiefly drinking – to alleviate his pain and later when the pain gradually diminished, to pass his time. One never knows when the devil enters the idle man, she thought. She kept a watch on him, not exactly prying on him, but by keeping a tab on his movements and actions. She took stock of their domestic property to ascertain if he took them away one by one to gamble. Valuables like the clock, the tape recorder, the black and white television, and then the not so valuable things from her kitchen.

She spent her work hours agonising over their future and when she got back home, pestered him with uneasy questions. 'Do you plan to spend your time this way? Or do you have plans to earn and feed us?'

She genuinely feared that he would get complacent and be satisfied with her paltry income that did not see them through even half the month. In her opinion, men took no time to get used to living off their wives' earnings.

'So what do you plan to do?' she demanded before dinner one day. She was determined to get a reply from him. No reply, no dinner, she declared. If he did not work, neither would she. Together they will starve and die. She had no desire to live this way.

It took a few minutes for Ramayya to answer.

'Do you have some money? I need some loan,' he asked expectantly.

She laughed derisively. 'Do you really think I have money enough to lend? From the three hundred rupees that I earn? We are living on debt already. I don't know when they will stop giving us things on credit in the shop. Once it stops, we will all eat and drink air.' She threw her hands up and breathed through her mouth for emphasis.

She hadn't meant to be sarcastic or rude, but she was beside herself with worry and her words were a mere expression of her undiluted apprehension. The children, their future, the probability of Ramayya falling into vices – the high-tide of angst within her threatened to breach her calm.

Ramayya felt as though she had jabbed a dagger into his heart. The outburst was so unlike her, so abrupt and harsh.

'And what exactly do you have in mind?' she asked. She had to know. What if he was planning to raise quick money from gambling or planning to put it into some venture that was sure to fail? He had friends who could waylay him with wrong advice and she had to be wary of any mishaps that usually accompanied the bad times in people's lives.

'I am not sure. But I am thinking of a few things. Forget it for now,' Ramayya said dismissively and continued to idle his time away.

Rukku worried over his intentions, questioning him in every way possible way to catch a hint.

'Imagine that I got you the money that you were asking for. What do you plan to do with it?'

Ramayya curved his lips and shrugged. It was a response that gave away almost nothing of what lurked in his mind. It would make no sense to disclose his plans now.

Rukku's angry salvos simply rolled off his back.

'Doesn't your pride hurt when you spend time doing nothing?'

Ramayya merely smiled and gave no answer.

'At this rate, it will become difficult for the children to go to school. We have to buy books and uniforms for the new school year. Or do one thing, stop their schooling and send them to work at the car garage.'

Ramayya nodded pensively and merely said, 'Why do you think so far? We will find some way.'

'Way? Which way? Does money just walk into the homes of the needy? You have to work for it, man.'

The stress of cleaning and scrubbing the house of other people's houses was getting to her, Ramayya thought and sighed. My poor wife, reduced to a maid, scouring over-burnt dishes, washing over-soiled clothes, and cleaning over-used toilets.

Sweeping office rooms was such an effortless thing to do in comparison.

The title of a sweeper somehow sounded better than that of a servant, which his wife presently held. There was at least no suggestion of subservience in the title he had formerly held.

'I have something in mind. It will be a while before I get down to doing it. Just allow me some time to decide. And if things go well, our bad times will come to an end soon.'

It was the best he could have said to placate her disquiet.

Two more unused, uneasy weeks passed in Ramayya's life.

Squatting outside the hill shrine, Ramayya felt the shaving knife skate across his scalp. The man in front of him worked deftly, making inroads on his graying head. Tufts of hair fell on his back and shoulder. The barber pulled the towel that had slid off his shoulder, wrapped it around him again. Through the corner of his eyes, Ramayya caught the other men and women in his vicinity subjecting themselves to a similar ritual of tonsuring their head. Within minutes they all emerged with a shiny, hairless pate, which was smeared with sandal paste for soothing, and their faces displayed a certain contentment of having made a sacred sacrifice. They had all given up their hair for the deity and the deity would now fulfill their wishes – both small and big.

Ramayya looked at them curiously, thinking what a great leveller complete baldness was. He was amused that the sandal coated pates made them all look so strikingly similar, like white pawns on a chessboard. He ran his hand over his head and felt the wetness of the sandal paste, pleased that he had made an auspicious start to his new life. He was beginning to put his new plans into gear.

He took his seat in the bus going downhill and as it wound its way down, surveyed the town below contemplatively. The view triggered a strange sense of apprehension in his stomach. He closed his eyes tight and offered a prayer.

✦✦✦

At home, he looked at the handheld mirror that his wife used while powdering her face and marking her forehead with vermillion. It wasn't the first time that he was shaving his head; he had done it many times as an offering to the deity, but the present occasion was different by dint of its purpose. It wasn't done to keep a holy vow like previous times. It was done as a first step towards making a fresh living.

Ramayya ran his hand on his head and felt the smoothness again. He tilted his head sideways and appraised himself again before running his finger over his moustache that begged to be trimmed and tamed. The moustache looked bizarre in the absence of hair on his head. Ramayya gave in to the plea of his facial hair, shaved and went to bathe. He felt his transformation in every sinew of his body and the thought of his new engagement with life filled him with a strange thrill.

In the bathroom as he rubbed the soap, he felt grateful for being a sparsely haired man as it spared him the ordeal of having to shave his body often. The removal of hair on his head and face were tasks he could not have escaped considering the demands of the new occupation.

Rukku had still not returned from her workplace and Ramayya was famished by the time he finished bathing. He waited for Rukku and for the food that she often brought home from the leftovers of her employer's lunch. It wasn't easy to accept the reality of eating someone's leftovers, but with time he had reconciled to the fact that in situations like these, hunger knew no pride, and every morsel that one got in charity was a blessing. At least until he got his feet back on firm ground again.

Ramayya stared into the mirror, catching the oddity of his face and marveling at the change that had come over him. It presented the image of a man newly emancipated from the travails of the past. In a moment of childish curiosity, he made faces – puckering and frowning and distorting – and then in another moment acquired a grave aspect and finally before putting the mirror away, slipped into a sobered look of satisfaction. He was embarking on a new pursuit that could leave the entire town in awe and their awe would make his future. He couldn't wait to get started.

He then looked at his body, as though to assess its appropriateness for the task he had decided to undertake. He wished he had a full length mirror for a more accurate estimation of his bulk but concluded that his lanky body was perfectly suited to the task. Even the small paunch that existed some time ago had vanished, tacitly endorsing his present condition – jobless, penniless, and living off his wife's measly earnings. There wasn't much scope to grow a paunch in such abject conditions.

It had been a long day of bone-aching, backbreaking work for Rukku.

Nevertheless, it was rewarding. She was taking home enough food for the whole family's dinner and she had earned twenty rupees as an incentive for the extra hours of work she had done.

Her employer's home was buzzing with wedding time activity. The daughter of the house was due to get married in a week and guests had begun to pour in. They ate, drank and changed clothes so excessively that Rukku was washing dishes and clothes for most part of the day. On her way home, she felt the roughness of her palms caused by soap and soda. She would have to rub oil in her palms and feet before going to sleep...and some balm on her back too.

She then thought of Ramayya with a feeble sense of disappointment. When would he return to his old working ways so that she would be spared of the responsibility of feeding him and her children? She had substantial displeasure about being a maidservant. It wasn't for this that her parents had married her to a factory worker, albeit a sweeper. They had scrimped and saved towards her dowry, ten sovereigns of gold and ten thousand rupees, and had given him an extra sum for his wedding clothes. All because he was a man with regular revenues capable of providing for his family. The ten thousand rupees had been long since spent and the gold jewellery had marched into the bureau of the pawnbroker in the wake of the crisis. It now seemed likely that it would stay there forever.

She thought of her children – a daughter and two sons – and felt worry pierce through her heart. Renu was fifteen and relations had already begun to enquire about her wedding. This would be her last year at school and as parents, they will have to be ready for her domestication. The thought triggered fears – about finding a suitable match (a factory worker preferably), about coughing up money for her dowry, about Ramayya's joblessness and about her sons' future.

'You are worrying too much unnecessarily. Everything will be all right soon,' she remembered Ramayya reiterating every time she voiced her concern. His quietude irked her.

All right soon, as though a fortune lottery was waiting to alter their fate.

What on earth could break his complacence? What did he have in mind after all?

While on one hand, Rukku was pleased that in the aftermath of his dismissal from work, he did not degenerate to a drinking, quarrelling, wife-beating maverick, on the other hand, she disapproved his idleness and lack of concern for their future.

There had to be an end to the uncertainty, and she would broach the subject at night, even if it threatened to end up in a verbal dual. She had to have a conversation even if it ended in threats of suicide and death. Even if it threw the house into a long spell of silence and gloom.

The door to the house was slightly ajar and the children had yet to return from school. Raghu and Ramu, who went to play football after school returned only after dusk and Renu came earlier. But today she wouldn't be home, thought Rukku; she had plans to go to her friend's house to get her hands coloured with henna and would not return before evening. The children's absence would provide the perfect opportunity to raise the issue with her husband.

'Are you there?' Rukku went in expecting Ramayya to respond if he was at home and awake. He had recently acquired a habit of sleeping for long hours during the day and pacing around home looking groggy and knocked out for the rest of the evening.

'I am right here. Why, it is past three. Late today? I am famished and am waiting for you to come.'

'What did you do with the rice and vegetables I had left on...Oh my God! What is this? Who are you?'

Rukku dropped her bag with the leftover food and gave off an alarm as she saw a silvery human figure speaking in her husband's voice.

'It is me, Rukku.'

Rukku stepped back in horror as the figure approached her with an air of distinct familiarity. The head was as bald as an egg; the body shimmering in silver had only a short silvery cloth around the waist. Stirring his eyes frenetically and baring his teeth in a genuine effort to smile (both of which only made him look more grotesque), Ramayya walked up to Rukku who stepped back further and stumbled upon a bucket of water, which toppled and spilled. The water took no time to merge with the spilled food to make an unseemly mix on the floor.

'It is me, Rukku,' Ramayya repeated, giving her a hand to get back on her feet.

Rukku's expression changed from one of horror to confusion. Avoiding Ramayya's hand, she gathered herself up, gazing all the while at him.

'What is this? What have you done to yourself? Have you then finally lost your mind? I knew this was going to happen someday. O God...'She gasped.

'I will explain it to you if you will let me. But I need your patience. Listen, listen... this is what I would look like for most part of the day from now on.' Ramayya said those words with an immediacy that bordered on desperation. He had to say it before Rukku began to clutter her thoughts with erroneous conclusions and began to wail.

Rukku looked on, startled, unable to decipher the deepening mystery of her husband's antic. She gave him a fresh onceover as if to ascertain that it indeed was him.

'Like this? Do you plan to break into people's homes in the night, frighten them, and loot their possessions? Upon your children, you will not do any such thing.'

Now, this was the problem with women. They had more mouths than ears, thought Ramayya, and swallowed his surging temptation to yell with frustration. Shut up and listen!

'Will you listen to me first? I am going to earn again, and this is my new look for the job,' he said maintaining calm.

Rukku sank on the wet floor again in disbelief. It was imminent, this insanity. She should have seen it coming. This is what long idle hours can do to a human being. Reckless, unwanted thoughts cloud the mind and create a fuddle, which ultimately lead to madness. Oh God, she thought. First he was only idle, now he is mad too. What would she do with him now? Who would marry the daughter of a mad man?

'Who do you think I look like now?' asked Ramayya, breaking gleefully into her thoughts.

'Eh?'

'Who do you think I look like now?' repeated Ramayya.

'A ghost,' said Rukku instantly. She was glad that the children weren't around to witness this ridiculous spectacle of their father strutting around in a ghostly form.

Ramayya frowned behind his painted face, and then reaching out to the table draw, took a pair of round spectacles.

'And now?'

Rukku stared, trying to make sense. A ghost with spectacles, that's what he looked like now, but she didn't say it. She merely shook her head.

'Don't you think I look like Gandhiji now?' asked Ramayya revealing his teeth in a proud grin. 'Wait for a moment.'

Ramayya then went in and brought with him a wooden pole (also painted silver) and holding it frontward adopted a stance that approximated a brisk stride frozen in action.

'Now, don't I look exactly like him?' he asked brimming with confidence.

Rukku wasn't certain, for she hadn't seen much of Gandhiji's pictures. She only had a vague notion, but she nodded her head, amazed at the novelty of her husband's idea of masquerading as Gandhiji and at the same time baffled at the inanity of his yet to be disclosed plan.

'But how will a fancy dress like this get you money?'

'That's what I am trying to tell you. This is no fancy dress. I am going to be the town's first and only live statue. Imagine the surprise of the people when they see Gandhiji's statue at different places. They will be so impressed that they will drop coins and even currency notes in front of me.

They will be overwhelmed by the patriotic sentiment that I will evoke in them, they will be moved by my unfailing, tireless endeavour, and they will not think twice before dropping money into the box.'

Seated on the wet floor, Rukku stared blankly at her husband. She felt the wetness spread on her bottom and unable to lift herself up from the new lash of disappointment from her husband, she shifted uncomfortably.

As Ramayya diligently displayed a variety of most commonly recognised postures of Gandhiji– in stride, waving, crossed legged on the floor – Rukku slipped into a swirl of thoughts.

Is this what he has planned for them? Is this what he called a job? This...beggary, or almost that?

From sweeping to cleaning to begging – their means of living were slipping down to pathetic levels.

Prodded by her thoughts she muttered almost unconsciously, loud enough for Ramayya to hear: A beggar's wife. Ten thousand rupees in dowry and ten sovereigns in gold. Only to see this day.

'Did you say a beggar? Me?' Ramayya said with a look of consternation.

He squeezed his eyes tight, clenched his teeth, and sucked air into his mouth. The skin on his face crumpled like a used leaf of aluminium foil. It was heart wrenching to realise that his wife perceived his new enterprise with such wretchedness. She did not see the honesty and ingenuity of his idea. What could be more wounding than this?

'What else would you call this? Expecting people to throw money in front of you for nothing,' said Rukku, still seized with disbelief and disappointment.

'It is not for nothing. I will be out there in the blazing sun at a time when even street dogs won't stray out, when the whole world looks for shaded spaces to escape the wrath of mid noon sun.'

Rukku heard him reiterate the decision he had made over weeks of joblessness.

He would be out there, in an almost motionless pose, like a statue, with only the blink of his eyes and thumping of his heart to suggest that he was human like all others.

He reiterated that he would not be evoking a wretched feeling in them, like seedy looking beggars in tattered clothes did. Instead, he would invoke their sense of nationalism, reminding them gently of the father of the nation and give a fair reason for them to reward him. Surely, his endeavour under the severity of summer and the ruthlessness of the rains will stir the conscience of even the most uncompassionate of men.

He said that he wasn't compromising his self-respect and asking for money. He said it once and then over and over again for a long time, until she realised that nothing could deter her man from carrying out his intention. He said it until Rukku understood and she consented, albeit half-heartedly.

However, even as the feeling of disgrace began to subside in her mind at the end of Ramayya's resolute arguments, another insidious emotion took position in her heart: fear.

The fear of a dehydrated, sun struck Ramayya collapsing and dying in some part of the town, and his corpse lying unattended until she went in search of her missing husband hours later. Rukku stiffened as a sudden grip of tension seized her body. She had to dissuade him from the adventure that he was embarking on with such blind enthusiasm. The embarrassment wasn't the issue now, his very well-being was. Wasn't this absolute madness, to embrace the harshness of the elements in the name of making a livelihood? Whoever gave him the idea?

'Will you not support me in this? Do you still think I am going out there to beg?' Ramayya said almost beseechingly before Rukku could voice her misgivings.

She took some moments to respond and then she stood up, letting the water drip down her saree.

She gazed into the unpainted, but pained eyes of her husband, and said softly, her face taut with concern, 'What if something happens to you? Have you thought about our fate in your absence? It frightens me to even think of it. Can't you do something else? There should be some other less demanding, less adventurous work, something normal, like all other people do. What makes you want to be a statue, of all things in the world? What an unthinkable thing to do.'

Ramayya smiled, tenderly, but with resolve. 'I want to do something that would make me a hero in the town that tainted my name and refused to give me work. A hero unlike any other so that those who called me thief would repent. What better way to prove my innocence than by taking on the guise of a man whom the whole world celebrates for his truthfulness?'

Ramayya spoke with such clarity and conviction that Rukku listened without uttering a word. There was not even a twitch of protest on her face. She recognised that his new enterprise had a sense of purpose and determination. There were tears in her eyes, there was admiration in her heart, and there was a new hope in their lives.

Fear and apprehension stepped back, and faith took over.

'Yes, I will support you...in whatever you decide to do.' said Rukku slowly, but firmly.

The initial days at work were faced with rigours of the kind that Ramayya had not even remotely anticipated. Apart from the sweltering summer, there were trivial troubles that demanded more than just mental resolve to contest.

Just when there was a group walking up to make an audience in front of him, gazing and smiling at him, touching him, provoking him to shift his stance, his skin would itch, sometimes in the most inappropriate spots. The sensation, which would begin as a minor tingling would then aggravate into an itch so irresistible that he would contemplate breaking the charade in the full view of the awed spectators and succumb to the frustrating urge unabashedly.

But breaking the act meant rendering his sense of purpose futile, that too in the most imprudent manner. He would rather die than do that, so he trained himself to resist the urge to scratch, as he did later with his urge to empty his bladder or take a quick slurp of water in the middle of the dumb charade. It was a formidable attempt, one that brought Ramayya to the brink of giving it up all together many times, times when he lurched back and forth between an unrelenting aspiration and a flagging will. It was a vexing contest of nerve and resolve that he had pushed himself into in order to seek a rare distinction for his nondescript existence and how much he loathed it at times.

Yet, he goaded himself on day after day, swathed in paint, to amuse the townsmen and tourists, until they stopped and began to take notice, watched in open-mouthed wonder, and dropped money in appreciation. And then slowly as days went by, as the money started gushing in, the agonies of the task diminished and he became the chosen subject for the people, the administrators, the politicians, and the media men to discuss.

The rigours became non-existent when eventually they turned him into the alter ego of the man whom they jointly revered and remembered as the father of the nation. They held commemorative functions on the leader's birth and death anniversaries and proffered veritable tributes in front of him.

Those were the special days of the year when the town honoured him in proxy, days when people marched up to him, garlanded him, and bowed reverently in front of him. The days when it was forgotten for some hours that he was a human being with a thumping heart, a growling stomach and a family back home surviving on the largesse of the admirers.

The adulation, no matter how chimerical, made the associated ordeals look negligible. What more could a labourer, who used to sweep and clean sprawling factory grounds once, and then was erroneously stamped a crook and dismissed, expect to achieve?

Even if his skin smarted under the summer blaze and his bare body shuddered in the monsoon, even if his throat withered and his eyes stung and blisters marred his body like potholes on the roads, even if wicked souls pinched his feet to test his resolve, he was completely content to watch from his frozen stance, a whole town falling at his feet twice a year.

In his view, it imparted meaning to what he did on the other days of the year.

It was that time of the year once again.

Ramayya took position in the children's park, this time sitting cross-legged, a little before daybreak and waited for the crowd – political leaders, district administrators, and schoolchildren– to arrive and celebrate Gandhiji's birthday.

A sweeper with the municipality walked into the park with an early morning look and began to clear the litter in the park – plastic bags, soda cans, water b24ottles, banana skins –yawning and muttering to himself. He was apparently piqued at being summoned to work so early in the day.

'Oh, you are here so early in the morning? Or did you sleep here last night?' he said to Ramayya, half mockingly.

He was one of those few in the town who knew Ramayya by name and identity. And then both being sweepers, there was the professional closeness that made their association something more than mere passing acquaintance. On weekends, it was him that Ramayya first met in the park, the man who interacted with him in the minutes before he transformed into a sculpture in flesh.

'Came in half an hour ago,' said Ramayya from his seat, taking out the spectacles and a book to hold in his hand from his rucksack. The collection box did not have a role on special occasions as these and he fully accepted the fact that he was there on these days to accept the tributes than to earn his routine proceeds.

The municipality man walked up to him and watched him curiously, as though to appraise and appreciate his likeness to the Mahatma in the country's history. 'I heard people say that you were going to be the ruling party's candidate in this year's assembly elections,' he said.

'The politicians now need me badly it seems. So why not use their need in our favour?' said Ramayya, a smile bordering on sarcasm breaking on his lips.

'Good for you. You will win, that is certain. There is no one in town that does not know you. You are very special to this town.'

'If you say so. I am only earning a livelihood just as you or anyone else is doing,' said Ramayya resignedly.

'Think of this. You will soon be a man with political power, mighty connections, and a lot of money. And then you will not have to be a statue.'

Ramayya thought about it and nodded. 'No, I won't have to.' He wondered if being a politician would be more trying and troublesome than being a passive, painted figurine.

The municipality man wedged the broomstick between his legs, lighted a cigarette, and said, 'Want one for an early morning kick?'

Ramayya shook his head. 'No, if people see me smoking I will lose the elections.' he said and smiled mischievously. 'I have new obligations now.'

The municipality man nodded meditatively and then inching closer to Ramayya asked, 'Will you do me a favour? After you win the elections, will you let me be the next Gandhiji of the town?'

Ramayya smiled inwardly as the irony of life nudged him gently and he raised his eyebrows. It was gratifying to recognise that he was getting his due from life, after all.

'Yes, I will,' said Ramayya after a moment's contemplation, like a patriarch bequeathing his prized asset to his favourite son. Like a king appointing his descendent. 'I will let you be my successor.'

He then raised his hand like a holy man and smiled. A sudden shade of vanity swept across his camouflaged face.

The municipality man threw the smouldering stub on the dewy, grassy ground, bowed gratefully, and walked away lugging the broom, pleased with the prospect of becoming the town's next father of the nation and then eventually transform into a power wielding, local politician.

He wouldn't be a sweeper for long, after all.

He smiled and walked out of the park, with the broom in tow.

Visit Visa

The bench by the creek on which she usually sat wasn't empty that day. She could see it from a distance, even in the grey evening light, with her cataract-ridden eyes.

The man was sitting upright, wearing glasses, and holding a book to his face. Neither a young lad nor a tottering old one, he was at an age when without the lenses all things at close quarters smudge into insignificance—an age when the world turns into a bowl of mashed potatoes without the reading glasses.

She demurred under her breath, her despise for the invader growing as she walked past the coffee shop where she paused every day to snort on the waft of pea berry fragrance. It was a routine, an indulgence that in a way helped her get over the feeling of deprivation that had set in soon after the homeopathy doctor had ticked coffee off her diet while prescribing medicines for her arthritis.

The murderous thoughts that had risen in her head that day for the doctor was identical to the thoughts she was beginning to get now for the man on the bench. How could someone trespass into her space unannounced like this? This was where she sat every day, watching people walk by engrossed in their own lives. This is where she revoked memories from the past, spread them out and sorted them all over again, separating the good from the bad, the thrills from the horrors, the smiles from the sniffles. This slotting of life experiences was her favourite pastime and at the end of the exercise, she would bundle them all up and bury it in her heart before walking back home as if life was all about watching maudlin soaps and serials on TV.

This haunt where she had private conversations with life was invaded by the man with the book that day. She had to get him out of there, but she had no inkling about how she would tell the man that the bench belonged to her.

'This is my place. Can you find somewhere else to sit?' she rehearsed it in her head and rolled her eyes.

That would be absurd. This place wasn't hers per se. But she had laid claim to it three years ago when her daughter and her family shifted to this locality near the waterfront. Surprisingly, every day, it was empty when she arrived, as if there was an unspoken agreement between her and the other visitors to the place that the bench was reserved for a woman to whom the bench was a sacred roosting place.

'It is not mine, but it is still mine. Not all things we own need to have our name on it,' she reasoned out as she strained her aching knee and tried to reach the bench urgently.

She didn't know how she would do it, but she had to shunt him out.

She felt sweat trickle down her temple which she quickly wiped with her sleeve. The wind was getting warmer with summer taking charge and she remembered her daughter cautioning her against the heat.

'Take water with you. And if you think it is hot, take it easy and stay home.'

But she had to walk every day for the sake of her knees and she was grateful for it. It gave her a pretext to live a life of her own for an hour or two. Those two hours were exclusive. The rest of the day was a miscellany.

The air sagged under a grey sky closing in on a sultry day. A collective drone of abras that ferried people across the creek echoed as a background to the tepid winds. It was intercepted by the sound of an airplane that had taken off from an airport nearby. She loved to watch the flight on an incline and made guesses about where they may be headed from the logo of the airline on its tail. It was yet another queer creek-side amusement of hers. But that day, she barely paid notice to the soaring aircraft or the buzz in the coffee shop behind the bench or the people milling about.

Before she realised it, she was standing on the empty side of the bench. The man paid no attention to her and was absorbed in his book. She caught a glimpse of the cover.

'Selected Poems by Gulzar.'

She stood on her aching knees, fidgeting, as if she were waiting for something promising to happen on its own, like the man walking away of his own accord sparing her the embarrassment of having to say ridiculous things. Unformed words quivered on her lips waiting to spill protest into the intruder's ears. But all she could summon up was a deep breath as a preamble to what she wanted to say. Defeated by her own nerves, she sat grimacing with pain. The involuntary groan made the man briefly look up and swiftly return to his book.

The sack of her past and its burden waited to be untied, the wares inside impatient to break free. But there was no way she could put them on display that day, not in the presence of a stranger. It would be akin to betraying her life, and no matter what life had handed out in her 60 years on this earth, she had an obligation to protect its honour.

The grouches were on one side, the gratitude on the other.

Wearily she picked herself, now encumbered with a cluttered life sack inside, and hobbled home.

'It's okay to sleep with the burdens one day,' she said to herself, turning to look one last time at the man and hoping it was only a wayfarer who would disappear with the day. If she found him the next day again, she knew she would do what was necessary. She had an entire night to plan a strategy to oust the man from her seat.

The next evening, she left home earlier than usual, with no specific plan in mind. For all the cross character scheming she watched in the serials, she wasn't proficient enough to take a cue from them and devise a plan when the need to be smart arose. Reaching early, before anyone had a chance to siege her real estate was the only thing she could think of.

'Ma, it is only 4.30 and extremely hot outside. What are you going to do so early?' her daughter Ananya asked as she took leave.

She didn't want to explain. She merely waved and said, 'I am not that old and frail, for God's sake. You treat me as if I am in my senile seventies. A little bit of arthritis and some bit of sugar, and of course, a stent somewhere in between does not old age make. Don't worry much about me. I will be alright.'

'Take your phone,'Ananya called out from behind, rolling her eyes and thrusting the phone in her hand with exasperation.

She didn't bother to tell Ananya how her castle had been invaded the previous day and she had to beat the invader to it by reaching there early. If he came back that is. She didn't think the story would be significant to Ananya. There were aspects of her life now that she didn't care to share with anyone. Not even her daughter. She prized her privacy and the ruminations she stacked it up with, immensely.

The coffee shop was abuzz with customers. She remembered it was Friday and business always picked up on the weekend. She had observed how people spent more time therefor conversation than for their beverage. She often wondered what it was that people talked to each other about, what it was that they laughed about so loudly. Friends, spouses, lovers – they were all there with someone who leavened their lives.

She saw the empty bench from that distance and heaved a sigh of relief. It was only late afternoon and there were no shadows falling on the bench in which she could take shelter. It was left fully exposed to the sunlight and if she had to secure her place, she had to bear the full brunt of its buffeting rays.

She considered taking a seat in the coffee shop and keeping a watch on the bench until light faded. But it was very vexing to think what she would do if the invader indeed arrived while she sat in the shop. The weather was against her, but she was determined to not let anything come between her and her treasured territory.

Six months of swelter to endure, she thought ruefully. It also meant six months of waiting for the return of the seagulls, her only companions in the evening in those months. When they were around, she often brought bread from home and fed them, and revelled in the frenzy they produced with their mobbing and squabbling. Now, the creek was quiet, its waters disrupted only by the abras going to and fro, with no other destination. Like her.

People had yet to start flowing into the waterfront promenade. Even as she sat secure in the thought that she had won her place back after all, there was a rankling sense of uncertainty rocking her heart. She had no clue about the source and cause of this unease, but it prevented her from opening her sack and spreading the stuff in front of her. Apart from that, there was little else she had to do sitting there and her state of forced idleness started getting to her, but she couldn't budge from there in the fear of losing her citadel. She closed her eyes and surrendered to the swelter in the air.

Suddenly she heard the noise of someone shuffling close to her and was startled to see the man with the book standing by the bench.

He gave a gentle nod, smiled and asked, 'May I?'

'Ye...yes... of course,' she stuttered and made as if to move and make room for him on the other side of the bench.

Rattled by the sudden entry of the man, she looked around frantically trying to find something to hinge her thoughts on. Something to settle her panic and rising anger. She wiped her face with her scarf and worried if sharing the bench would now become regular. She pressed hard on the ground beneath her feet and wondered if her world was beginning to come apart.

'It's a very hot day,' the man said, pulling out a handkerchief from his pocket and wiping his brows and neck. He had the same book as the previous day in his hand.

She merely nodded in agreement.

'Do you come here every day?' he asked.

She nodded again marking a feeble 'yes.'

She didn't want him to talk to her any further. She despised him wholeheartedly for his act of transgression, but at the same time she was surprised that he talked to a stranger with such ease and air of familiarity. It was not common in this desert city of dreams. People were generally gentle, but not friendly. No one smiled at passers-by and strangers on the street. It was as if smiles were in short supply these days.

It had taken a long time for her to come to terms with this indifference of people, especially after having lived in Mumbai all her life, where even amidst the rigours of life people took time to smile and greet. They loved more easily than they did here. There was a fluid comfort in being part of the crowd that was constantly on the move, trying to get somewhere from somewhere.

She suddenly noticed that the man was talking to her and felt a twinge of guilt at not having paid attention. As if to make amends, she smiled at him and asked, 'Do you live here?'

She was eager to know if his visits will only be temporary and he will not make 'reading by the creek' a permanent fixture.

'Not really. I live in India. I am a doctor. I am here for a month, on a visit. I reached only three days ago.'

He must be in his mid-sixties, she calculated. His face was long, with a pointed chin which was covered in a neatly trimmed beard, and a broad forehead over which fell a lump of hair. Rarely did men have such a flourish of hair at this age. The salt and pepper shade added grace to what she now thought was an amiable face which carried two prominent lines down from his nose. The high cheekbones gave an impression of a fixed smile that seemed to touch the corner of his eyes.

He must have been a handsome man in his youth, she surmised.

'It's a nice place,' he said. 'Although the heat can rob a big part of the reading pleasure.'

She nodded again.

'Do you read poetry?'

'No... not really.'

'I am a fan of poetry more than any other form of literature. It brings you closer to the finer things in life, you know. There is no better way to go to sleep than reading a few verses. I picked this up at the airport.'

'Gulzar,' she said in acknowledgement. 'His songs are all that I am familiar with. I like them.'

'Of course! Who doesn't? Ek akela ek sheher main, raat aur dopahar mein...Which is your favourite Gulzar song?'

She felt vexed. She hadn't expected him to ask her this. She was vaguely familiar with songs by Gulzar but did not have a thorough knowledge of his repertoire. But Aandhi was her favourite movie and she had learned Tere bina zindagi by heart several decades ago. She said so. She was not inclined to sound more erudite or poetically inclined than she was actually.

'Cult movie, indeed. Suchitra Sen looked beautiful.' And after a pause during which he leafed through the book, he asked, 'Here's something that I read yesterday. I would like to share it with you. Poetry becomes more beautiful when it is shared. Can I?'

She looked up at him curiously. She was astounded by the liberty he was taking with her. She also realised that she was letting him take the said liberty by engaging him in a conversation that she had no reason to indulge in. But she was bored with her own lacklustre world, and there was a feeble sense of relief when she mentally consented to let a Gulzar poem turn the key and open the doors to something fresh in her life.

'Yes, it will be nice. I only hope I will understand. I don't understand poetry much. Especially if it is Urdu.' she said sheepishly.

He let out a little laugh. The lines on his face deepened.

'Don't try to understand poetry. Just feel it. And it will make sense on its own.'

She looked into the distance and smiled. A touch of yellow from the setting sun flickered in her eye. She had long since stopped making sense of anything. Her life lived on its own, for its own sake.

'*Arz kiya hai...*' he said, calling her attention.

'*Yaad hai ek din*

Meri mez pe baithe-baithe,

Cigarette ki dibiya par tum ne,

Chote se poudhe ka ek sketch banaya tha.

Aakar dekho, us paudhe par phool aaya hai.'

'Can you read it again?' she asked eagerly. And then seeing him looking askance at her, she gave a gentle laugh and said, 'Of course, I understood. I just want to hear it again.'

He read the little verse about flowers blooming on an inert plant sketch again. She liked the way he intoned the lines in his deep, resonant voice. It brought the verse alive. Then he read some more, carefully choosing verses which had less of Urdu words, and wherever there was one, he paused to translate. And before she could begin to admire his knowledge of Urdu, he tapped on the book and confessed with a boyish grin.

'All the poems are translated here.'

He was a funny man, she thought. The intruder who read verses to her unsolicited, and made a difference to the grey, summer evening as if it was endorsed by nature itself. And then as she looked at him to take leave, she observed his hands shivering slightly. The book wasn't steady in his hands. Parkinson's was slowly staking a claim on his life. It was a somber discovery for her.

Later that evening she asked Ananya if Parkinson's could kill people sooner than they would otherwise. There was an unusual disquiet in her voice.

'It depends,' said Ananya. Some people live even up to 20 years after diagnosis. 'Why?'

She didn't reply. She merely nodded as if to say, well, that's promising. She allowed herself to heave an imperceptible sigh without questioning its import.

'Why did you ask? Is anything the matter? Are you alright?' Ananya asked, a wee concerned, to which she got only an affirmative nod.

Ananya was used to her mother's irresponsive nature. She was also by now used to her rapidly growing silence and the tendency to ask random questions out of nowhere. Many didn't even warrant a reply. They were mere thoughts that had found a loud escape. She acknowledged that for all that her mother had endured in her life, she deserved her space, and there were unstated boundaries that she had set which Ananya made no attempt to violate.

Later that night, as the last of the TV soaps ended, she Googled for 'poems of Gulzar' on her phone and searched for the one on the table sketch. She couldn't get over it. Failing to find it on the net, she quickly read a few others and she felt her eyes drooping shortly. Not much made sense in that state of partial slumber, but she knew that she had found a new interest in life. Poetry.

The unexpected drizzle could have stopped her from going out to the creek side any other day. How much can change in an evening! The grouchiness that had rankled her two days ago had sobered and in its place was a sense of placid ease. There was something more than the solitary unscrambling of the past that her outings promised her now.

Armed with an umbrella, she walked out again wondering how the parched earth must have felt when the rain fell. She wondered why it never rained for long in these places. The drizzle, if at all it sustained, would become a quick downpour and even before the ground had soaked its abundance, the skies became dry again. But then she thought, even the desert gets its share of rain. There was solace in that passing contemplation.

She wasn't certain that her new companion by the creek would return today. Children tended to stop the older folks from venturing out alone in any kind of weather. It is either too hot or too windy or rainy or there is virus in the air. It was possible that he will be stopped from stepping out, given the unstable weather.

If the man didn't show up, she had her bag of the past for company, in any case. She hadn't opened them in two days, and she worried they may feel betrayed. If she didn't give them their due weightage, they will eventually desert her, making her life bereft of even its solitude.

The drizzle, as expected, didn't transform into a rain. But it lent a fragrance to the evening air, although it had become stifling and heavy with moisture. She folded the umbrella, felt its soothing dampness in her palm for a moment and then used it to wipe the seat before settling in. She gave the sky a sweeping glance and wondered where all the clouds that had gathered only a while ago had gone. They had dissipated from wherever they had come from, without falling on the ground.

'Searching for the clouds?' she heard the baritone from behind her.

She turned around and greeted the man with a quick smile.

'Some rains at last,' she said.

'Actually, no. A rain is real only when it falls. These are just passing clouds and not all clouds need to rain,' he said coming around and taking his place.

She wasn't sure she understood the full import of what he had just said, but it sounded beautiful. 'A rain is real only when it falls.'

'Is that Gulzar?' she asked curiously.

He chuckled. 'Did it sound that good?'

'It was good, of course.'

'Thank you,' he said with a conceding grin.

'Did you write it?'She asked, not believing what she had inferred.

He nodded, his grin still in place.

'Arun Sharma. Doctor by profession, poet at heart. Age 68. Single. Ready to mingle and make friends.'

She stared at him, unable to make sense of his jaunty introduction.

'If you feel I am not a total stranger anymore...' his voice trailed off.

'Err...yes, I mean, no, of course....Jay...Jayshri...Agarwal.'

She didn't feel the need to declare her age. She wondered if she looked older than 62, and suddenly becoming conscious, she ran her hand over her short, hennaed hair.

When he put his hand out briskly, the tremor in it was visible. She hesitated, her hand now resting gently between her neck and shoulder. Surprised and unprepared, she put her palms together quickly and said a namaste. She wondered if he might have felt slighted at her refusal to reciprocate his friendly gesture. He raised an eyebrow and gave a quick nod in recognition of her reluctance, withdrew his hand as if it didn't matter and returned her formal greeting. His ease of manner and acceptance surprised her again.

Moments passed in complete awareness of the silence that had crept in between them. She waited for him to say something, wondering if he was waiting for her to break the ice. There was no better way to start a conversation than by mentioning the weather, and so she said off-handedly, 'This drizzle is going to increase the heat.'

It was such a lame thing to say, but she was pleased that she had made sufficient amends for the unrequited handshake by speaking something. After having lived in an ivory tower for long, with limited associations and acquaintances, it was difficult for her to break free and be amiable at once to someone she barely knew. But she now felt a feeble interest to know more about him. He was single, he had said, which meant he was a widower. And a doctor, which could mean anything from being a pediatrician to cardiologist.

'Are you with your children here?' she sounded mildly curious.

'No...no. With my nephew and his family. And you?'

'I live with my daughter and her family.'

'You are lucky. I mean, to live with and be surrounded by your own people in old age is a blessing.'

She looked at him quizzically.

'Ask someone like me who wakes up to silent walls and have only the ghazal singer's or the news reader's voice to go to sleep with.'

'But isn't it liberating? Having no one to question you or make you feel obliged or to nag you with silly do's and don'ts. To live on your terms?'

'Jayshriji, it's sometimes good to have someone to nag you in life. Too much of freedom will make one redundant to oneself. You know what I mean? Lonely. Wasted. Unwanted.'

'Those words describe me too,' she said, trying hard not to betray any emotion.

He smiled. And she smiled too. Two geriatric smiles that conveyed two different feelings of deprivation melded with the air.

In the weeks that followed, they learnt a lot more about each other than they would have initially expected to know. At least, she was amazed at the ease with which she opened her sack of the past and presented some of its most unpleasant scraps to him. She spoke about her abusive, loveless marriage in which she chose to remain until her daughter came of age and stepped out of home, taking her along to wherever life might take them. She said how asphyxiated she felt in her daughter's home. Grateful though for all that her only child had done for her yet feeling indebted and restrained. She regretted being a burden on her daughter.

'Sharma ji, I don't want you to misunderstand her. She is the most dutiful daughter one can have. It's me. I feel guilty of being an intrusion in their life. I don't feel a part of their set-up. It's frustrating to be lonely in a crowd.'

He listened intently, never eager to interrupt with a question or an advice. Which was worse, he wondered—to be lonely by oneself or to be lonely in a crowd?

There was a lull before she suddenly brightened up and asked, 'What's your story, Sharma ji?'

He gave off a gentle laugh and shook his head. 'What story can an old, unmarried man have?'

'Why? That's a story by itself. You being unmarried. Tell me about it.'

Her change of manner from that of a brooding elderly woman to that of a juvenile bubbling with curiosity took him by surprise. She, on the other hand, was amused at her temerity to wangle out personal details of his life and realised that there was something about his presence that made her feel emotionally secure. Something that she hadn't felt even with her daughter.

'Nothing much, Jayshri ji. It's an old love story gone awry,' he said dismissively looking up at some reluctant bits of clouds that came down and stopped abruptly. Strangely, neither of them felt the need to seek shelter and allowed the drizzle to punctuate their life stories.

'I was a spineless jerk who couldn't get his girl.'

She waited for him to continue without prodding further.

'I was only sixteen and had no clue about what life was, but believed that there was nothing in this world like being in love. But you don't get a girl but merely being in love. You had to be eligible enough to stake your claim in front of the girl's father. And I was only a student.'

'So?'

'So her father got her married off to some rich man of equal status in the town. And I became a Devdas.'

'You mean you remained unmarried all your life for that girl?' she asked incredulously amidst her laughter.

'Yes. I never found anyone quite like her after that and I didn't want to waste my life with anyone else.'

She stood up, her laughter now reduced to a mischievous grin. 'No wonder you became a poet. I won't ask you if you tried to know her whereabouts thereafter.'

'It is useless to know. When you have let something go, it's gone. Forever.' With that he too rose to go. She noticed his face turn briefly solemn, as if a vestige of an old woe had just trotted across his usually cheerful countenance.

Just as love had myriad hues, its lacking too had different shades. Hers was one, his another.

Before parting at the road crossing and going their different ways, he announced he was leaving for India the next Friday.

'Which is, day after tomorrow, Sharma ji! And you are telling me now?' She looked hurt at the abrupt and casual manner in which he had shared the information. The fact that the day was almost upon them upset her.

'What difference does it make if I told you now or earlier?'

She chose not to reply. Before crossing the road when the pedestrian crossing light turned green, she asked in a very matter of fact tone. 'Will we meet again?'

'I will be here tomorrow,' was all he said in reply.

She was irked with herself for the dejection that had surfaced in her heart at the news of his departure. It was an unnecessary emotion, one which made her deeply aware of the old and new privations in her life.

Later that night, she thought of the girl for whose sake Mr. Sharma had forsaken the conjugal joys of life and had slithered into an old age which carried her residue. She wondered if the man the girl had married would have loved her as much as Mr. Sharma or if he would have turned out to be a wife-beater like her own husband. For her own satisfaction, she chose to believe that the girl's life couldn't have been any better than hers. It gives comfort to trick the mind into thinking that suffering and sadness was equal among human beings, and no one was more privileged than the other.

In a very curious fashion, deep in her heart she relished the thought of the girl not having Mr. Sharma in her life.

Jayshri woke up the next day with a swelling in her kneecap and was barely able to get on her feet. She received an earful from Ananya to whom her mother's slightest discomfort was a crisis. She always felt overly indebted to her mother for the sacrifices she had made for her sake and felt burdened by it. Strangely, she felt guilty about enjoying the good things in her life, especially when her mother lived in the shadows of her past, eschewing merriment, and settling into a permanent state of depression. She had wished that her mother had found newer joys and fresh directions in her life after she quit her marriage. There was enough scope for it, but unfortunately, she had chosen to wallow in her woes than to escape its melancholy.

'Do you really have to stretch yourself so much? Why don't you stay home if you aren't feeling up to it? You never listen to what I say and look who's suffering now.'

'Me.'

'No, it's me too with you.'

'Why do you borrow my difficulties? Why don't you lead your life your way and let me lead mine? Put me in a senior citizen's home.'

'Ugh...Ma, don't start off again.'

Ananya could never explain it. Her love for her mother was also the cause of her frustrations. If only her mother had been happier in life, if only she could do something to change the past, if only she could make the present different for her mother. But somehow, they had all settled into a murky space of inexplicable unease with each other and there seemed no way out of it.

'We will go to the doctor in the evening after I return from work.'

'Not today.'

'Can you tell me why? Do you want to wait till the swelling increases to the size of a football? Be ready. I will come by six.'

The silence that the house drowned in after Ananya, her husband and the children was marred by the weeping and wailing on the TV. Jayshri regretted not having taken Mr. Sharma's phone number. It was somehow not deemed necessary at that time.

After spending the entire morning in restlessness and layers of orthopedic cream on the knee, she decided that the doctor could wait. It wouldn't please Ananya to find the house locked when she returned from work, but certain things had to go the way she wanted, Jayshri thought determinedly. If nothing, her newfound friendship with Mr. Sharma warranted a proper good bye, and no pain in the knee nor the obdurate orders of a daughter could alter that.

At five in the evening, she stepped out of the building, ruing the increasing humidity in the air, and waited for a taxi. Wary of Ananya suddenly appearing in front of her, she hid behind a large SUV till a taxi came by and took her to the creek. What would happen on her return home was something she did not wish to contemplate, but she knew that this trip of hers was worth any drama that she may have to face later. She felt buoyed by her ability to defy someone else's bidding. What had kept her from doing it in all those years of marriage, she still didn't know.

For the first time in many weeks, she found the bench occupied when she arrived. She saw from behind a young couple with their arms around each other's shoulders, deeply engrossed in conversation. She did not wish to intrude into their space but having no choice she went and stood within their sight in the hope that they may make some room for her. But people in love are oblivious to the woes of the world around them. Unable to bear the pain in her knee, she asked them hesitantly if she could sit.

The couple moved a little and she smiled tentatively as if to say both 'sorry' and 'thanks'. It wasn't easy to sit next to a dating couple and pretend you weren't interested in them, but she tried hard not to eavesdrop or pry from the corner of her eyes. She was amused that the world still fell in love after all the instances of betrayals and break-ups it had seen time and again. People still made promises. Kissed. Made love. And lived happily-ever-after? That she didn't know.

Mr. Sharma was later than usual that day. While waiting for him she randomly thought of the day she had first seen him on the bench, her heart bursting with despise for the man who had invaded what she believed was her sole territory. She also acknowledged with a gentle smile that the bitterness had gradually diluted and ceased to exist. Once he leaves tomorrow, he would once again become a 'nobody' to her.

When she suggested that they find another bench, he asked if she would like to have a coffee. She had almost said to him that coffee was forbidden to her, when it occurred to her that it was her day of singular decisions.

Their conversation that began over two cups of latte bearing foamy patterns on its surface lasted long into the evening, well after the sun had set beyond the creek. He showed her the new smart phone his nephew had got him and confessed that he had very little clue about how to use it. It was an unnecessary addition to his life, he said. He was happy with his old Nokia.

She then taught him a few things that she knew. Like kids exploring a new toy together, they played with it, laughing over their ignorance, and berating the new world that made life more and more complicated. They had things to say long after the coffee had cooled and got consumed. They even had a mock quarrel over who would pay for the coffee.

And just as they prepared to exit the coffee shop, he held out a notebook with black and white stripes, and a page marker sticking somewhere from between the pages. Before she could assume that he had got her a present and made a protestation, he said, 'My poems. They were written over many years and were scattered over two-three old diaries. I made a fair copy in the leisure time I had here, more to beat boredom than with any specific purpose. I have no use for it. I thought I could give it to you.'

She felt a sudden sting of tear in her eye. 'I...I am honoured, Sharmaji. I don't know what to say.' she said leafing through the book and catching a glimpse of the hand-written verses in them. 'But, why me?'

'I didn't meet anyone worthy of it in all these years. And I didn't want to give it to anyone who didn't deserve it.'

She gave him a smile, and gently touching his trembling hand, said, 'I haven't been this happy in a very long time. Thank you.'

On her way home, in the cab, she wondered if they would meet again. She had not asked him, even if perfunctorily, when he would visit again. Along with it, it occurred to her that she had forgotten to take his mobile number once again.

As they approached the red light, she asked the driver if they could return to where he had picked her. What if he was still around, leaving memories to linger long after he departed?

'There is no U-turn here, Madam,' said the driver, stopping at the red light.

She nodded and turned to look at the road she had left behind.

'A road with no U-turn,' she said, with a warm, wistful smile.

About The Author

Asha Iyer Kumar is an author, poet, and active blogger based in Dubai. She has been an Opinion page columnist, feature writer and editorial consultant with *Khaleej Times*, Dubai, writing on LIFE for several years, and is now a creative writing coach and mentor for children and a youth motivational speaker. She made her literary debut in 2009 with a novel, *Sandstorms, Summer Rains* and published a book of verse, *Hymns from the Heart*, in 2014. Her short story, *Free Spirit*, was published in the anthology, *The Other*, edited by Mona Verma and Abha Iyengar in 2018.

Her other books are as follows –

Hymns from the Heart (Poetry, 2015)

Let it be, Love (Short stories, 2018)

Life is an emoji (Collection of essays, 2020)

That Pain in the Womb (Short Stories, 2021)

Sandstorms, Summer Rains (Novel, 2022)